**A Degrassi Book**

*Maya*

**A Degrassi Book**

# Maya

Kathryn Ellis

James Lorimer & Company, Publishers
Toronto, 1992

Cover photo: Janet Webb

**Canadian Cataloguing in Publication Data**

Ellis, Kathryn, 1955-
  Maya

(Degrassi ; 20)
ISBN 1-55028-363-4 (boards)
ISBN 1-55028-361-8 (pbk.)

I. Title II. Series

PS8559.L558M3 1991 jC813'.54 C92-093185-5
PZ7.E55Ma 1991

James Lorimer & Company, Publishers
Egerton Ryerson Memorial Building
35 Britain Street
Toronto, Ontario
M5A 1R7

Printed in Canada

This book is based on characters and stories from the television series *Degrassi Junior High/Degrassi High*. The series was created by Linda Schuyler and Kit Hood for Playing With Time Inc., with Yan Moore as supervising writer.

Playing With Time Inc. acknowledges with thanks the writers who, with enthusiasm and dedication wrote the original scripts upon which this original story is based — Yan Moore, Susin Nielsen and Kathryn Ellis.

The author would like to thank all those who offered their expertise and advice, especially The Spina Bifida and Hydrocephalus Association of Ontario.

# Chapter 1

"What is it that makes sixteen seem so special?" Maya wondered aloud.

"It's 'cause we're old enough for everything, now," replied her best friend Caitlin, who was draped lazily on the swing on Maya's front porch. "We're old enough for jobs, we're old enough to drive, we're old enough for life — finally!"

Maya, sitting in her wheelchair next to Caitlin, took another sip from her glass of pink lemonade. She didn't know what it was, but pink lemonade always tasted better to her than the regular kind. It tasted like summer.

And summer it was, the very first day of it, and all stretching out in front of her, her summer of being sixteen.

"Caitlin, we have to make a pact," said Maya, leaning forward. "This summer, we'll get jobs, we'll get our licenses. Think of the freedom — my mom won't have to drive me everywhere any more."

"It's a deal," said Caitlin.

"And boyfriends!" Maya concluded.

"Boyfriends, definitely boyfriends," Caitlin agreed.


Maya wheeled into the house to get the morning's paper. There wasn't much they could do about boyfriends at this moment, and driving lessons were going to cost money, so it seemed that jobs would have to be the first priority. For Maya, of course, there was also the not-so-small matter of having the family van adapted so that she could drive it. Having been born with spina bifida, she didn't have enough sensation or strength in her legs to work the pedals, and she would need to have manual controls in order to drive the van. She wondered how much it would cost.

The girls turned to the Help Wanted section and began to skim through the ads.

"Want to be a bricklayer?" joked Caitlin.

"I suspect we're not qualified," Maya smiled back.

"Okay, here's one," said Caitlin. " 'Attractive salespeople required for clothing store. Experience preferred.' We sold a lot of chocolate bars in the Unicef fund raising this year. We're experienced."

"Okay, put a mark by that one," agreed Maya.

2

The girls continued to pore over the pages, Maya's long tangle of dark hair almost touching Caitlin's sleek honey-coloured hair. "Oh, listen to this," exclaimed Maya. " 'Yorktown Village now hiring guides, cashiers.' Do you think we'd get to wear those old-fashioned clothes? It'd be so much fun!"

"Let's apply to that one first," said Caitlin.

A quick phone call netted them both interviews for the following day. At dinner that night, Maya was dying to tell her family the exciting news.

Maya's parents were both terrific cooks, and tonight Maya's mom had made a wonderful cioppino, a stew of various kinds of fish with tomatoes and herbs. When they all had steaming bowls and slices of fresh crusty bread at their places, Maya finally couldn't wait any more.

"Guess what," she announced, pausing to get everyone's attention. "Tomorrow, I have an interview for a job at Yorktown Village."

"As what, a farm animal?" asked Maya's younger sister, Janna.

"Janna!" reprimanded their mother.

"I was just kidding," answered Janna, sullenly, slurping her cioppino.

"What do you mean, 'an interview for a job'?" asked Maya's father.

"What do you mean, 'what do you mean an interview for a job'?" asked Maya, surprised. "An interview for a job," she reiterated.

"What do you need a job for?" asked her father. "We can afford everything you need. You get an allowance for treats."

"It's not the same," said Maya, hearing a dangerously whiny note in her own voice. She tried to sound more rational. "I want to earn money so I can take driving lessons."

"Driving lessons!" exclaimed her mom. "You're much too young to be driving."

"I am not, I'm sixteen. I'm old enough to work, and I'm old enough to drive. And I'll pay for the lessons myself."

"I don't want you driving. You're not nearly mature enough," said her mother flatly.

"Besides, you can't drive the regular van, anyway," pointed out her father, gently.

"You can get it adapted, and it can still get switched over so you guys can drive it," said Maya, trying to sound sensible, but knowing she sounded childish and cross. "I checked today." Maya glanced at her grandmother, her Bubbie, who usually took her side in things, but she was busy helping five-year-old Joel with his supper.

"And how much does that cost?" asked her father.

4

"Five hundred dollars, around," Maya muttered.

"Five hundred dollars!" exclaimed her father, and then went on more gently. "Maya, I know I make a good living, but this family has a lot of expenses." It seemed a little unfair that just a minute ago, he'd said that she had enough money, but she knew better than to take that line of argument with her dad. "And, I agree with your mother, I'm not sure you're mature enough to drive just yet. Can we leave it for now — maybe pursue this a little later?"

Maya looked down at her cioppino, tearing her bread into smaller and smaller pieces. It wasn't fair. If she were Caitlin, her parents wouldn't have to deal with things like the cost of converting the van. Right now, Caitlin's parents were probably smiling and driving her down to get her three-sixty-five, as the kids called the Learner's Permit. And it wasn't fair that her parents still treated her like a baby, even if she was acting like one now, pouting into her stew. She was sixteen, for heaven's sake!

Fortunately, Joel suddenly remembered a hilarious riddle he had heard at the playground earlier on. "Hey!" he shouted. "What lies at the bottom of the ocean and twitches?" When no one answered imme-

5

diately, he screeched, "A nervous wreck!"

All the adults laughed uproariously, while Maya replied, "Joel do you have to scream so loud?" and Janna muttered, "That's so old." But both sisters smiled a bit, and the tension was broken.

After the dishes were loaded into the dishwasher, Maya went to her room and pulled out her notebook, like she always did when she was upset, but she couldn't think of a thing to write. It seemed like she was out of luck on the driving front, but the question of her getting a job had been left unresolved. It was hardly material for a poem.

As she stared at the page in front of her, she heard a soft tap at her door. "Come in," she called, flipping onto her back and pulling herself up into a sitting position.

Bubbie poked her head around the door. Maya beckoned her to come in and take a seat on the foot of the bed.

"Why do you want a job?" You had to say this about Bubbie, she always got straight to the point. "You don't need one, you could just have fun this summer."

"Everyone else gets summer jobs, Bubbie," Maya replied.

"And if everyone jumps off a cliff, you do it too?" asked Bubbie. Even though Bubbie had come to Canada when she was a

6

young girl, you could still hear a trace of the old country in the way she spoke.

"No, Bubbie," said Maya. "But they're not jumping off a cliff. They're getting a job, they're being independent. I want to do it, too. And if I could drive … " Maya sighed wistfully. "I'd just like to feel more — more normal, sometimes."

"So talk to your mom and daddy about it," urged Bubbie.

"I did — you saw what happened."

"You have to do it right. You have to see it their way first — then you can make them see it your way."

Maya looked at her grandmother again. What was she trying to say?

"Why don't your parents want you to drive?" Bubbie asked her.

"They say I'm not mature enough," answered Maya, and then she stopped. "Oh, I get it. I have to prove I'm mature. But how?"

"Isn't there another reason they don't want you to drive?"

Maya thought a moment. "The money to convert the van." Then, suddenly, the solution was obvious. She smiled at Bubbie. "*I* earn the money to have the van converted. Then how can they say no?"

"You're a smart girl, my *shayna maidl*," said Bubbie, patting Maya's hand. "Just like your Bubbie."

"But mom will never drive me to a job interview," said Maya, shaking her head.

"Take a taxi. I'll give you the money."

Maya opened her mouth to protest, but Bubbie held up her hand. "No, you'll pay me back when you get the job."

"Thank you," Maya smiled.

Maya was dressed her best. She had brushed her unruly hair back into a ponytail and tied it with a gold ribbon. A pair of linen-look beige pants was topped by a short-sleeved ivory T-shirt with gold buttons along the left shoulder. She had even polished her tan leather shoes, despite the fact that, using a wheelchair, Maya never scuffed them. Large gold hoops and a small gold Star of David on a chain, that she almost always wore, completed her outfit.

Caitlin had convinced her to put on a little pink lipgloss and some mascara, even though neither girl usually wore much makeup. Caitlin was being interviewed right now, and Maya leafed nervously through a brochure about Yorktown Village. The room was full of teenagers also waiting to be interviewed, and though they tried to be subtle about it, Maya knew they were looking curiously at her wheelchair. She kept her head down and pretended not to notice. Maybe it was stupid to have come out here to be interviewed. Probably her parents would be furious if they found out, and there was no way they were going to hire a kid in a wheelchair anyway. And the taxi had cost nine dollars, just to get here. How would she get to work every day? She couldn't afford a job!

Besides that, there was the interview. What would they ask her? What would the right answers be?

The door in front of her opened, and Caitlin emerged. Before Maya could ask her how it had gone and what they had asked, she heard her own name being called.

"Right here," she replied, and buzzed herself toward the door.

"Good luck," Caitlin whispered after her, but Maya didn't really hear her. She was looking at the woman who had called her name, looking at the expression on her face. It was obvious she wasn't going to get the job, and it was because of her wheelchair. The door closed behind them.

"Maya, I'm Betty Sorrento."

"Nice to meet you," replied Maya, nervously licking her lips. The lipgloss tasted slightly sweet, a little like strawberries. Or pink lemonade.

"Maya, I hadn't realized when I spoke to you on the phone that you used a wheelchair."

9

"Is it a problem?" Maya felt a little angry, but she wasn't going to let it show. Eighteen dollars down the drain, by the time she paid for the taxi home.

"No, of course not, we're an equal opportunity employer," said Betty Sorrento. "It's just that I don't think we have any suitable openings at this time — we've filled the cashier openings already, and as for the guides ... " Betty Sorrento shrugged. "You see, Yorktown Village is set up as a town would have been over a hundred years ago. We've made sure it's accessible to our visitors, but we like to keep things as authentic as possible. There just weren't any electric wheelchairs in those days."

"I also have a manual chair — or maybe you have one of the kind they used in the olden days."

"I'm sorry," said Betty Sorrento. "Our costumed guides have to be able to weed the herb garden, lead a cow to the barn, churn butter, all the things that people did in those days. I don't think you'd be able to do that."

"They had disabled people in the olden days, I could be representing that. It might be interesting for people to see. I could be knitting or something. I know how to knit."

"Dear, I understand that you want the

10

job, but I'm afraid we just can't hire people who can't manage all the parts of the job — we don't have the budget. Besides, life was very hard for disabled people in the nineteenth century. I'd be afraid I'd be putting you in danger. I'm sorry, but I'm sure you'll find something suitable in a more modern environment. You seem like a very bright girl. Thank you for coming in for an interview."

Maya could see there was no point in arguing with her. She just nodded and turned to go. She felt disgusted, disappointed and angry. What a waste of time, what a waste of money. She knew she shouldn't let on how she felt, that she should remain polite and friendly. She half-smiled. But she couldn't quite bring herself to say thank you.

## Chapter 2

"It's so unfair!" complained Caitlin as they shared the cab home together. "It's prejudice, is what it is."

"I can see her point, though," said Maya. "I mean, why should they pay me to do only part of the job?"

"Oh, you're being so good," said Caitlin. "I wish I had your patience. I was really looking forward to working there together, too. Maybe I should refuse the job, in protest."

"Don't," soothed Maya. She couldn't believe she was the one soothing Caitlin. After all, it was Caitlin who was going to get to wear the long dress and the crisp white apron and little white cap and learn how to churn butter and all that other neat stuff. And it was Maya who was out the taxi money and didn't have a job. But it was sweet of Caitlin to be upset. "Don't. You'll have fun, and I'll come down and

12

laugh at you in the silly outfit and everything. I'll get another job. We'd get sick of each other if we saw each other every day anyway."

Since they saw each other every day in the school year, they both knew this was ridiculous, but Caitlin let it pass.

But getting another job didn't turn out to be so easy. She tried the clothing store that had advertised, but they weren't even as nice as Betty Sorrento. She applied for an office job, but then she had to phone them from downstairs to cancel the interview — they were on the second floor and there was no elevator. She couldn't reach the grill to be a short-order cook, and she didn't waste her time applying to be a bicycle courier, a window-washer or a lifeguard. And then there were the three or four promising interviews that ended with the interviewer saying, "We'll call you." And then they didn't. Maya was starting to get depressed.

It wasn't like she hadn't expected life to throw her a few curves, Maya mused, while sitting with her favourite pink lemonade on the front porch, alone this time. She had run across prejudice and misunderstandings before, and though it was sometimes hard, she had learned to roll with the punches. But she believed, she really did, that most people wanted to do the right thing. So why wouldn't they hire her to do something she knew she could do?

"Maya!" It was Caitlin calling to her as she ran up the walk. "I couldn't wait to show you — I got my three-sixty-five! I start my lessons next week!"

Oh, wonderful. Maya smiled wanly at her friend.

"Come on, I'm taking you to Slurps to buy you a milkshake," announced Caitlin. "It's a celebration."

"I don't know," Maya began, but then she thought, come on, this is your best friend. If you can't be happy for her happiness, you're not much of a friend. "Let me tell Bubbie I'll be out."

Slurps was not far from where the girls lived, just about a block from Degrassi High, and a lot of the kids hung out there after school. It was a fun and funky hamburger joint with a real old-fashioned juke box that somebody always had a quarter to throw into, and it was done up in a fifties style, in pinks and turquoises and chrome. It was strictly counter service, but that meant you could pretty much hang out as long as you wanted without getting thrown out, as long as you didn't get rowdy. This original store had been so successful that it had expanded into a citywide chain, and Slurps were now opening up in some of the neighbouring cities, like Mississauga, Oshawa and Barrie.

Although there were often kids they knew in Slurps, today there was no one that they knew more than just to say hi to. The girls got their milkshakes, Maya's strawberry and Caitlin's coffee, and settled themselves at one of the tables.

"Was the test hard?" Maya asked Caitlin about the written test that led to the Learner's Permit.

"Not too hard," said Caitlin. "I got mixed up on a couple of things, but most of it was pretty much common sense. I can't wait to start driving! Just think, you and I could cruise out to someone's cottage, or to a nice beach somewhere, go to Montreal for the weekend, stuff like that."

"I wish I could go for my three-sixty-five, but there's not much point until I can afford to get the van converted," said Maya ruefully.

"How's the job hunt going?" Caitlin asked her.

"Not great," admitted Maya. "I'm running out of possibilities. It's like people don't quite believe I can do anything. It's really frustrating."

"That's so stupid," said Caitlin, indignantly. "People should know better than that. It makes me so mad."

Normally, Maya would have jumped in and calmed Caitlin down, but she felt too dejected to bother.

"I feel like my whole summer's shot down," said Maya. "No job, no license, no guys, no sweet sixteen."

"Oh, come on, Maya, cheer up, you'll find something," encouraged Caitlin. She paused to take a sip from her milkshake. "You know what you *could* do," Caitlin said, suddenly.

Maya looked up.

"You could do some kind of volunteer work. I know there's no money in it, but it would prove that you can do something, and then you could put it for 'Experience' on the application form."

Maya was disappointed in Caitlin's suggestion. She wanted money — not to be greedy, but the whole point was to get to drive. "I suppose," she said grudgingly, and abandoned the topic. Right now she didn't really want advice, she just wanted to feel sorry for herself. "It *is* unfair," said Maya. *"You've* got a job. *You've* got your three-sixty-five. At least you don't have a boyfriend yet."

"Right," agreed Caitlin, looking quickly into her milkshake.

"You — don't, do you?" asked Maya, hesitatingly, knowing what the answer was going to be.

"No. No, I don't have a boyfriend," was Caitlin's answer.

"But there's a guy, right?"

Caitlin stirred the last of her shake with her straw. "Well, there's sort of a guy. Nothing has happened yet, though. Probably nothing will."

A little gossip could always bring Maya out of herself. As long as it wasn't some creep like that Claude guy Caitlin had gone out with last fall. She smiled in anticipation. "Do tell," she encouraged.

Caitlin was obviously dying to talk about him. Maya had to give her credit for not flaunting it before now. "Well," she said, giggling a little, "his name is David, he's a blacksmith's assistant at Yorktown Village, so you can imagine he has a great bod. He's ... got brown hair, blue eyes ... really cute. He always waves when I go by the blacksmith shop, and says, 'What, ho! Miss Caitlin,' and I don't think it's just for the tourists. He's exactly my type."

"He sounds wonderful," agreed Maya. "Now where am I going to find my type?"

"Describe your type," said Caitlin.

"Okay," said Maya, leaning forward and getting into it. "He's tall, and nice, and funny, and ... " Maya didn't know where to go from there.

"What does he look like?" asked Caitlin.

Maya's eyes roamed around the restau-

17

rant, and landed on the short-order cook shaking a basket of fries behind the grill. "He might look kind of like that," she said, indicating the cook, tall, with long dark hair tied up, and a serious expression on his face. As Caitlin turned to look, Maya hissed, "No, don't let him see us staring. I just meant kind of like that."

Caitlin casually brushed a napkin to the floor and, turning to retrieve it, glanced around the restaurant.

"Maya, I didn't know you went for the hairnet type," teased Caitlin.

Maya, to her own surprise, blushed.

That night, in bed, Maya thought about her job hunt again, and her boy hunt. There was no way she'd ever get a boyfriend if she just sat around on the front porch all day, and anyway, it was really boring with Caitlin off at work all the time. Her other friends were all working or away this summer, too — or both. Diana had gone to visit family in Greece for the summer, and Melanie was being a camp counsellor up north all summer. Kathleen was working in the library, but Maya didn't like Kathleen much anyway. She did know other kids at school, but not all that well. There were the boys, but Maya didn't really feel right calling up a boy to do something, and anyway, Arthur and Yankou and Yick were such *children* (well, Yick was sort of cute). No, if she weren't going to die of boredom this summer, she *had* to get a job. Plus, with the money came the van conversion, and driving lessons, and FREEDOM! Plus, she might meet a guy where she worked.

But on the other hand, how was she going to get to work? She didn't think getting her mom to drive her was quite the answer, since she wasn't all that keen on Maya working anyway. And she'd heard that WheelTrans could be dicey sometimes. And if she took cabs, she'd burn up her earnings so fast … she'd already gone deep into her savings just going to the fruitless job interviews. The only way it was going to work was if she could find a job she could get to on her own.

But it looked like no one was going to give her a job anyway. Maya was slowly drifting into sleep, listening to all these thoughts and restless images pursuing themselves endlessly through her mind. A van, a milkshake, the guy from Slurps. Her eyes popped open. Slurps. It was close to home. Maybe she could apply there.

Next morning, Maya waited impatiently for people to get out of the house. Mrs. Goldberg and her mother finally went off shopping, and Maya was left to keep an eye on Joel and Janna, who were playing in the back yard. Maya used the phone in Bubbie's room to call Slurps Head Office. She had already decided that if she could present a job to her parents as a *fait accompli*, they'd probably say yes.

"Slurps, how can I help you?" came a voice at the other end of the line.

"Um, yes, could I have the personnel department, please?" said Maya.

"One moment." Goopy music played for a moment or two, and then another voice came on the line.

"Personnel, Nancy speaking," said the voice.

"Hello, do you have any summer job openings?" asked Maya.

"We're always taking applications," Nancy replied. "We get openings from time to time. Can you come in tomorrow? You could fill out an application and we could interview you, at — oh — two o'clock?"

"Perfect," said Maya. As she set down the phone, she realized that she had a very good feeling about this.

# Chapter 3

Despite all Maya's careful planning to have everything be mature and rational the next evening, dinner was turning into a disaster. Tonight, they were having one of Maya's favourites, tacos. That was where the trouble had started.

"Mm — mom, tacos, my favourite," Maya had exclaimed when she had come to the table.

"Oh, Maya, whenever I cook dinner I try to make something nice, and your favourite is *tacos*, that come out of a box?" was her mother's response. "I only made them because I didn't have time to do something *nice*."

Oops. "Well, I meant they're my favourite when you have to do something quick." Whew! Smooth recovery, Maya, she congratulated herself. Too soon.

"Well, I wouldn't have had to do something quick if I got any help around here," her mother snapped. "Where were you all afternoon, anyway?"

Maya glanced at Bubbie. Bubbie didn't know she'd gone to the job interview, but she probably guessed. Would she have an ally in her grandmother? Should she wait until her mom was in a better mood before she mentioned it? Bubbie nodded back, very slightly, encouraging. Right. If she was supposed to be acting mature, she'd better not blow it by starting to tell lies.

"I went to a job interview … and I got the job!" said Maya.

"What?!?" came her mother's reply. But before she could say anything else, two things happened. Joel, who had been quietly loading spoonful after spoonful of the tempting salsa onto his taco, bit into his dinner, and screamed, spitting the fiery mouthful onto his plate. Janna's taco shell split down the back as she bit into hers, spilling ground beef, tomatoes, avocado, lettuce, and salsa onto the floor, and she burst into tears.

Bubbie was busily getting Joel calmed down with a glass of water that he was too hysterical to drink, and Mrs. Goldberg said something astonishingly close to swearing before heading to the kitchen for a cloth to mop Janna's spill. Mr. Goldberg was soothing Janna's tears, and Maya just sat there, torn between dismay and amusement at the reaction her announcement seemed to have caused.

It took a few minutes for everything to get settled down, Janna and Joel with fresh tacos, and Maya decided it was probably a good thing, because her mother seemed to have forgotten about Maya's announcement.

"What sort of a job?" asked Maya's father, in a perfectly matter-of-fact tone of voice.

"At Slurps," said Maya, "the one near Degrassi. I can get there by myself. I'm on the counter taking orders."

Maya's mom and dad looked at each other for a moment. Her mom spoke first.

"Honey, I'm not sure it's such a good idea. You don't really need a job, and it seems like so much trouble."

Maya felt disappointment inside, a feeling like a stone dropping into a well. Bubbie gave her a steady gaze, seemingly trying to send some kind of mental message. Maya took a breath.

"I would like to have a job," she replied calmly to her mother. "I would like to earn my own money, and I'd like the responsibility. I can get to work on my own, and I promise I'll still do my chores around the house. It was hard to find a job, you know. I think I should be allowed to try to do it."

The Goldberg parents exchanged that

look again, and then Maya's father smiled.

"Well, good for you," said Mr. Goldberg. "When do you start?"

Bubbie winked at Maya across the table.

It felt really strange to Maya to be in her favourite hangout, but on the other side of the counter. When she had arrived, she had asked the girl behind the counter to see the manager. The girl had lifted a section of the counter like a drawbridge, and Maya had wheeled through. It was a whole new perspective on Slurps. You could see all the seats from the counter, and watch people come through the door. Since it was just ten o'clock, there was only one person having a cup of coffee, a guy reading a newspaper by the window.

"I'm Sarah Anne," the girl was saying. "You must be the new girl."

"Yes, I'm Maya," said Maya. Sarah Anne was petite and very pretty. Her black hair was braided into tiny cornrows elaborately arranged, each ending in a glass bead. Her dark skin glowed like silk or polished wood, and a pair of painted parrots hung from her ears.

"I'll take you to meet Scotty," Sarah Anne was saying. "This way."

Maya followed Sarah Anne through the shining stainless steel kitchen. The grills were spotless, utensils hanging from

24

hooks near them, french fry boxes were stacked high on upper shelves. A group of people, all around Maya's age, was chatting as they busily chopped onions, tomatoes and lettuce with huge knives. Everything seemed big, and copious. Where at home you might put a little mustard in a dish, here it was a mixing bowl-full. Giant jars of pickles and mayonnaise lined the shelves, and buns were stacked in flats along one wall.

They passed out of the kitchen into a long corridor. Maya caught a glimpse of a storage room with shelves full of paper cups and boxes, and a cupboard that contained some big string mops and seemed to have a sink in the floor. Soon, they were in a small, untidy office with walls covered in rec room-type wood paneling. A youngish man in a navy suit, with movie-star perfect teeth, smiled at her across a pile of papers.

"Ah! You must be Maya Goldberg! Welcome to Slurps. Sarah Anne, thank you, you'd better get back out front."

Maya smiled. She wasn't sure what to say. But she didn't have to worry, because Scotty just kept going. "I'm Iain MacFarland, but everyone calls me Scotty — I'm sure you can guess why, by my accent." It was true, he had said something like 'Slaairrps' for 'Slurps'. But his accent wasn't that strong, really. Everyone here was so friendly. Maya had the feeling she was going to like it.

"Well, Maya, let's get you into a uniform." Scotty crossed to a green metal cupboard on one side of the room, and opened it up. Inside, Maya could see several striped tunics like the one Sarah Anne was wearing, hanging crookedly on wire hangers. "We like you to wear the tunic — if it's cold you can wear a long-sleeved top underneath — and your own pair of plain pants or skirt," explained Scotty. "The tunics you leave behind each day, and they get washed. They each have a number, so you wear the same one each time. The visors, I'm afraid you have to buy — health regulations, you know. Now, let's see, what size would you be?" Scotty looked Maya up and down. "Well, you're not so tall, let's try you in a medium."

Scotty handed her the tunic and a visor. "You can get changed in the washroom just here," he explained, leading her to the employees' lounge next to his office. "After you're dressed, we'll fill in some forms, and then I'll get Kirk to show you the ropes."

The lounge was also covered in rec room paneling — Maya suspected it was just nailed to the wood framing. In the women's washroom, off the main lounge, there were two stalls and two sinks. Fortunately, there was a little bit of space beside one of the sinks, or Maya wouldn't have been able to reach the taps in her wheelchair. At least there was a wheelchair-accessible cubicle. Above the sinks was a long mirror, cracked in one spot, and missing its silvering in patches. Maya was struck by the contrast between the gleaming public areas and kitchen, while the staff areas, though adequate, were kind of cobbled together. Still, she figured it didn't pay Slurps to sink a lot of money into the parts of the restaurant the public would never see.

Now, Maya turned her attention to the tunic she was to wear. Although Maya had of course seen the uniform hundreds of times before, she'd never really noticed it. It could have been a lot worse, she supposed, but it wasn't the sort of thing she would have chosen to wear. It buttoned up the front (which was merciful, since she always had trouble with back zippers in the wheelchair), with big, turquoise, cloth-covered buttons and pocket flaps the same colour. It was fitted to her waist, then flared out over her hips. The main part of the tunic was white, with pink and turquoise stripes, but the turquoise wasn't quite the same shade as the buttons and pocket flaps. It was short-sleeved and collarless. Maya checked herself in the mirror, pulled on the matching visor, and went back to Scotty's office.

"Maya, this is Kirk," Scotty said, and Maya turned pink. It was the short-order cook she'd noticed that day with Caitlin, not yet in uniform.

Without his hairnet, he was even more gorgeous. He was tall — six feet, maybe, thought Maya. His hair was long, past his shoulders, dark, like Maya's, only sleeker, and he wore it tied back. He had an oval face, and sparkling, kind eyes that you had to look to see, and he looked like he really, actually had to shave (regularly — not at this exact moment!). He was dressed in a black leather jacket with a few small chains on it, a crisp white shirt with the top two buttons open, and black denim jeans. His belt seemed to have some sort of fancy silver buckle, but she didn't like to stare too closely at some guy's belt buckle, and she thought he was wearing boots, but whether motorcycle or cowboy, she couldn't quite tell out of the edge of her eye. He had a small gold hoop in one ear.

"Hi, Maya," he said. His voice was light, dusty, not too low, but quiet.

"Hi, Kirk," Maya's usually husky voice sounding huskier than normal. Oh, no, Maya, don't let on. Then, again, he hasn't heard you talk before, what does he know?

"Kirk, get in uniform, then I'd like you to show Maya the ropes, please," said Scotty, with a gleaming smile. "And *try* to be on time in future."

"Aye, aye, sir," Kirk replied, with a salute and a grin. Then, more seriously, "Sorry."

By the time Maya had filled in the employment forms, Kirk was back, wearing his hairnet topped by a two-pointed cap, and a masculine version of the tunic the girls wore, with a long, white apron over top. The two of them went out to the kitchen.

"Okay," Kirk was saying. "I know you're going to be working out front, but it's good to know what goes on back here. Oh. I'm sort of a shift manager — I'm in charge when Scotty's not here. Now, when someone places an order, we get it here, and clip them up on the string. This way they get served in order — we just slide them along. All the burgers and stuff stay in this freezer here, and they get cooked on the charcoal grills — that's why they taste so good. This is the condiment table — everybody, this is Maya, she's new, Maya, this is Tommy, Kei-Kei, Grace and Shazia, don't worry, you'll catch on to all the names eventually."

A friendly chorus of "hi's" was exchanged. A pretty blonde girl, who seemed to be the one called Grace, also said "Good morning, Kirk," in a sort of flirty voice. Kirk smiled back at her, and then steered Maya to the other side of the restaurant kitchen.

"Now, here's where we make the fries and onion rings, and fish and chicken sandwiches, all in the oil. That gets changed regularly. Buns are here, as you can see. All the stuff like cups, straws and napkins is back here," Kirk continued, leading Maya into the storeroom, and indicating the shelves where each item was stored. "When we're slow, we do stuff like make up the french fry boxes. One day last summer it rained so hard we had about two customers and made enough boxes to last the rest of the summer!"

Maya smiled, but she was already overwhelmed by all this information. Finally, Kirk led her out to the order counter. "This is where you'll be — you've met Sarah Anne?" Maya nodded.

"Okay, when you take an order, you write it on one of these pads, then you put it in this slot and yell 'Order in!' What's your uniform number?"

"What?" was Maya's response. "My uniform number?" Why on earth did he suddenly ask her that?

"Yeah, you know, may I?" he said, gesturing toward the back of her neck. This was getting stranger and stranger. She just nodded, having no idea what she'd just agreed to. Kirk reached out and, tucking his finger in the back of her uniform, pulled up the tag. Maya didn't breathe. But his finger never touched her skin. "Sixty-four," he announced, and tucked the tag back. "This is the uniform you wear every day. To make it easier, you put that number on your order, here," he showed her a box on the order form. "Then, when it's ready, we yell, 'Order up sixty-four!', and then you know yours is ready."

"Oh," said Maya, thinking she sort of understood it.

"Don't worry," Kirk assured her, "you'll catch on."

Maya could only hope he was right.

"Okay, now, if they order a burger, you have to ask them what they want on it, and put it on the order, too," Kirk was saying.

Sarah Anne broke in. "They always ask you what their choices are. It's ketchup-lettucemayomustardonionpicklesrelish-tomatoes, cheese is twenty cents extra. Just write the first letters on the top of the pad, you'll catch on."

So everyone kept telling her. Sarah Anne walked her through it. "Okay, K for ketchup, L for lettuce, two M's for mayo

31

and mustard, O, onions, P, pickles, R and T, relish and tomatoes." Maya dutifully wrote them down on the top of the pad, the part that didn't tear away when she would tear off an order.

"Perfect," said Kirk. "Now, you guys do drinks unless it gets really crazy out here, then call one of us. Coffee is here, the brown pot is regular, the orange is decaf. Coke, orange, Sprite, here, just press the cup against the big bar. If you want water, press the little bar at the back of the orange, for club soda, press the little bar on the Sprite. Milkshakes and ice-cream you can learn later. Okay?"

Maya felt almost dizzy at this non-stop superspeed training session. "I'll catch on," she said, having learned at least that part of the ritual.

"Good for you," smiled Kirk, and again, she noticed his kind eyes, that you had to look to see. "Only one more thing to learn, and that's the cash. It's quite simple, really. Everything has its own button, you just press it. You'll catch on to where they all are. The machine knows the prices and the taxes, and it goes into our inventory computer. If you make a mistake, press Cancel, here. Then press Total, which appears up here. Then, when the person gives you the money, press the amount in, and it tells you the change. Set the money here on the ledge until the person checks their change, in case there's a disagreement. You can open the till by pressing this button — " Ching! The drawer under the counter popped open. "Try to put the money all facing the same way, it's easier to count. Ready to start?"

Maya smiled, and as she said, "I'll catch on," Sarah Anne and Kirk chorused, "You'll catch on."

"Thank you," said Maya.

"Any questions, ask Sarah Anne or me." And with another sparkle of his kind eyes, Kirk was gone.

"Here comes your first customer," said Sarah Anne. "Are you ready?"

"I'll do my best," said Maya, smiling up at the young woman who had just come into the restaurant.

# Chapter 4

By the time the busy period during lunch was over, Maya was exhausted, and she still had four hours before she could go home. Kirk came out of the kitchen and told her she could go on break — her lunch would be at 1:30 each day that she worked — and she gratefully headed for the staff lounge. Maya had brought her own lunch that day, not sure what the policy would be about food, and was munching her tuna sandwich while leafing through an old music magazine someone had left behind, when Kirk walked in.

"Hi, mind if I join you?" he asked in his quiet, dusty voice.

Mind? Mind? Maya would have *paid* him to join her. "No, not at all," she replied, in what she hoped sounded like a casual tone of voice.

Kirk flopped down on the beaten-up vinyl sofa and unwrapped a hamburger. "I hate it when I get lunch in a restaurant and I have to cook it myself," he said with a smile. "And pay for it too. At least I'm a good tipper."

Maya laughed. Kirk was the kind of guy that would normally intimidate her — tall, good-looking, too cool to have the time of day for a girl in a wheelchair — but here he was, joking with her and putting her at ease on her first day.

"There's a picnic table out back you can eat lunch at on nice days," he told her. "How's it going so far?"

"Pretty good," said Maya. "The lunchtime rush was a little overwhelming. I couldn't remember what the 'O' stood for on my pad, and offered someone olives instead of onions, but luckily they didn't want any. I think I gave someone regular coffee instead of decaf, they'll probably wonder what hit them this afternoon. Otherwise, okay. I think I'm catching on."

"Good," said Kirk, reaching for his drink.

"Have you had a lot of other people who work here that use wheelchairs?" Maya asked.

"No, why?" said Kirk.

"I don't know, everybody is so calm about it, no one stares or seems to get nervous. It's eerie."

"Why would we do that?"

"Any new place I go, I always get a little

of it," explained Maya.

Kirk shrugged. "Well, we knew you were coming. We just want to make you feel at home. We're a good bunch here, I like to think. But we can all go weird if you want us to."

Maya smiled. "No. I like it the way it is." She glanced at her watch. "Oh, shoot, I'd better get back out there."

"See you later," said Kirk, picking up Maya's discarded magazine.

"Lucky you," said Sarah Anne, when Maya returned to her post.

"What?"

"Your lunch overlaps with Kirk's. Lucky you."

Maya wasn't quite sure what to say, but Sarah Anne was still talking.

"Well, don't you think he's sort of cute?"

"He's all right," said Maya — the understatement of the year, she thought. "But he must have a girlfriend, or something, doesn't he?"

Sarah Anne gave Maya an arch look with an exaggerated shrug. "Who knows?" she replied. "I don't think so, but he's always Señor Mysterioso. I can tell you a couple of people around here who wouldn't mind," she grinned.

Although Maya knew Sarah Anne was talking about herself, and probably Grace, and who knew, maybe even Shazia, for the second time today, she found herself turning pink.

"Oh, Caitlin, I'm so tired, but it was great!" Maya was on the kitchen phone with the door closed, while the rest of her family watched TV in the living room. "But I didn't know work was going to be so exhausting!"

"Don't worry," said Caitlin, "you'll get used to it. I was a wreck for the first week, I didn't know how they could have *lived* in those days — churning butter is like the twenty-minute workout! But I'm fine now."

"That's good," said Maya, with relief. "But anyway, the reason I called you is, remember the guy, the cook I pointed out the other day?"

"Mr. Hairnet," said Caitlin.

"Call him whatever you like, everyone in the kitchen has to wear one," said Maya, "Without the hairnet he looks great — wears his hair in a ponytail — and he's my boss, sort of. Caitlin he is *such* a hunk! And he's really nice — he has gorgeous eyes. I hope I dream about him tonight. Every night."

"Why dream?" laughed Caitlin. "You should get him for real."

"Give me a break," said Maya, suddenly coming back to earth. "You think a guy like him's going to be interested in the wheelchair poster girl?"

"I thought we had a pact," said Caitlin. "We were both going to get boyfriends. You can't wimp out now."

"Boyfriends, sure. But a guy like that — he could have anyone. Probably does. I think I'd better set my sights a little more realistically." Maya sighed. "But it sure would be nice."

"Well, what makes you think a creep is going to go for you any more than a hunk would? And why would you want him if he did?"

"I don't mean a creep. Something in between," explained Maya.

"Maya, there's the best, and there's the rest. Go for the best."

"How's David?" asked Maya, suddenly tired of the topic.

"He's fine," said Caitlin, in a giggly voice.

"Come on, cough it up."

"He's taking me out on Friday night. We're going to a movie. Hey, are you working Friday night? We could come by Slurps, and you could meet him."

"No, I'm on the day shift. But I'm off Saturday — perq in the first week — I won't get that too often. Come over Saturday and tell me everything."

"It's a date," Caitlin replied. "Gotta go, my dad wants the phone."

As Caitlin had predicted, Maya did get used to the job, and all the work. After a few days a lot of things started to become routine, and she didn't need to think about them any more, which made it easier. She learned the list of condiments, and soon memorized where each item was on the cash register. She started to get to know the others — sweet, little Sarah Anne; Tommy and Kei-Kei, who were like a comedy team at times; Grace, flirty, show-offy, but fun; and down-to-earth Shazia. Kirk never said too much during work, but he was part of the gang, while still overseeing the shift.

Scotty was a friendly boss, and chatted with them all at least once a day, his smile always a million watts. Sometimes Maya found him a little overbearing, his sense of humour a little sarcastic. Sometimes she felt there was some double meaning to his jokes that she wasn't getting. Sometimes she was pretty sure she did, like one day when he came up to her while she was wiping down the counter, and said, "If I said you had a beautiful body, would you hold it against me?" Maya knew it was an old Groucho Marx line, she'd seen the movie on late night TV once. But when Groucho said it, it was funnier. She tried to smile, realizing she was probably just being oversensitive. She knew she didn't have a beautiful body. Sure, like most girls with spina bifida, she was pretty well-developed on top, but she wasn't all neatly proportioned, like the models in magazines. How could she be, with little-used leg muscles, and a curve in her spine that threw off her posture? She could live with it — she didn't have much choice — but she didn't like having it drawn to her attention. Still, Scotty probably just hadn't thought about it from her point of view.

A nicer thing was that the lunch schedule from the first day was actually permanent — she had lunch overlapping Kirk's every day. She wondered if she was just replacing someone else's lunch, or if he'd planned it that way. The other half of Kirk's lunch overlapped with Kei-Kei's, so it didn't tell her much.

By the end of her first week, Maya and Kirk were becoming friends. Maya found out that Kirk had been out of school for a year, working full-time at Slurps.

"Didn't you want to finish school?" asked Maya in surprise. Kirk was a dropout?

"I finished Grade Twelve," Kirk replied.

"But — " Maya didn't want to offend him, she didn't quite know how to phrase her question. "Don't you want to be something when you grow up?" Well, that couldn't have sounded much stupider. But Kirk didn't seem to take offence.

"I am grown up," he smiled at her. "This is it." Then he shook his head. "I was never much good at school. I like the real world, earning money, better. Maybe someday I'll have my own restaurant."

To Maya, university-bound all her life, this sounded incredibly strange, but when she thought about it, she couldn't help admiring Kirk for going with his own strengths. She tried to picture Kirk in the future.

"That'd be cool," she acknowledged. "I can see you, in the kitchen, wearing a chef's hat. White linen table cloths, candles and flowers on the tables, and you're cooking up coq au vin, or something, flambéeing away in the kitchen." It started to seem almost romantic.

"You have a great imagination," Kirk laughed. "I was thinking more of the sort of place that's open all night, and all the most interesting characters in town drop by. We'd do burgers and stuff, but we'd also serve the best seafood in town, whatever was caught fresh that day … spaghetti alla vongole … seafood gumbo … deep-fried calamari … fricassee of rubber boot … "

Maya knew it wouldn't progress to anything more, probably, but those short lunch breaks were what she looked forward to most each day. Kirk's quiet charm, his understated sense of humour, the way he treated her like a regular person. There was no patronizing, or pity, or weirdness about her being in a wheelchair. There was no talking down from an eighteen to a sixteen-year-old. It was just ... natural.

So Maya finished her first week, tired but happy, and looking forward to Monday, when she'd see Kirk again.

Maya was sitting in her porch swing this time, when Caitlin came up the walk.

"This will be rare, us both having Saturday off," Caitlin remarked. "Let's do something."

"Like what?" asked Maya.

"I don't know. We could go to the mall. I'd like to get some new sandals. Do you need anything?"

"I don't want to spend any money. I've got to save up for the van conversion. But I'll come with you."

Fortunately, the mall was close enough that Maya could go in her wheelchair. She transferred from the swing to her chair, and as they went along the sidewalk, Maya asked Caitlin about her date with David.

"Oh, it was great," said Caitlin. "He picked me up in his dad's car — very fancy, with those windows that roll down by pressing a button, you know?"

"So you spent the evening rolling windows up and down?" asked Maya.

"Of course not, I was just telling you it was very elegant," protested Caitlin. "Anyway, we went to the movies, we saw *Edward Scissorhands*, Maya, you have to go and see it, it's so romantic. Then we went out for a Coke after, and then he took me home."

"Did he kiss you goodnight?" Maya wanted to know.

"Just a little kiss, very gentlemanly," Caitlin assured her.

A ripple of jealousy washed through Maya, but she kept smiling. All the guys went for Caitlin, she was so pretty, so perfect, smart but not intimidating, petite, such delicate colouring, everyone wanted to look after her. She'd had boyfriends ever since Grade Seven when she started hanging out with Rick, and then there was Joey, and the guy she went to the nuclear plant with, Robert or something, and Arthur had that big crush on her, and Claude — the list seemed endless. And here was Maya, the old cliché — sweet sixteen and never been kissed.

"What did you talk about?" asked Maya.

"Oh, stuff, work, the movie, each other. I gotta tell you, though, you would have loved the movie. Johnny Depp was really good, he was this misfit guy, with scissors instead of hands, and he cut all these bushes into shapes — " Suddenly Caitlin stopped, and looked at Maya. "I think I really like David," she said. "He's really — I don't know — sort of romantic. I mean, I could picture him doing what Edward Scissorhands does at the end of the movie — but I don't want to give it away. Actually, David looks a little like him, except without cuts all over his face, of course. Really soulful eyes."

"Yeah," sighed Maya, thinking of Kirk's eyes. They weren't big and soulful like Johnny Depp's. You might walk past Kirk on the street and not notice his eyes, but if you took the time to stop and look, there was something so warm in them, sort of vulnerable and strong at the same time, something you could trust.

The girls continued on in silence, each enveloped in her own romantic pink cloud.

Finally, Monday rolled around, and Maya set off for work, looking forward to seeing Kirk again. So what if it was just a fantasy? At least she was friends with him. Maya's crush had turned into a sort of fever over the weekend. She hadn't been able to think of anything much but Kirk. He was absolutely perfect, kind, thoughtful, funny, but also delicious, delicious to look at, to be around. If only he could feel that way about her.

He was friendly and said hi when she arrived, and then, as usual, he joined her on his lunch break.

"Have a good weekend?" he asked her, flopping on the sofa in the staff lounge.

"Not bad," she answered nonchalantly. "You?"

"As good as can be expected, considering it wasn't a pay week."

"What did you do?"

"Oh, not much. Worked on my car. But I need money before I can go much farther."

"You have a car?" asked Maya in surprise. "How come you never drive it to work?"

"Well, that's why I need the money," he explained. "It doesn't run, yet. But when it does, pow! Freedom!" He slid one hand across the other, like a car laying rubber.

"Yeah, freedom," echoed Maya. "As soon as I have enough money, I'm going to get our family's van converted so I can learn to drive. It'll be great. I can't even take transit or ride a bike, like able-bodied people can. But what kind of a car is it?"

"Well, it's kind of a mongrel," Kirk admitted. "It's mostly a seventy-five Impala, ugly as a warthog, big as an ocean liner. Some of the parts are kind of creatively worked in. Chewing gum, string, tin foil."

Seeing Maya's incredulous look, he laughed. "Just kidding."

"I guess I'll have to learn about cars if I'm going to drive," said Maya. "Maybe you can teach me someday."

"Sure, why not?" agreed Kirk.

Just then Scotty came in, and he'd obviously overheard part of their conversation.

"Gonna let her see what's under the hood, are you?" he asked Kirk. "That's a good one."

Kirk looked uncomfortable, and Maya felt hot. Why did Scotty have to come in and ruin a perfectly nice moment?

# Chapter 5

By Friday, Maya felt completely at home at Slurps. At lunch, she and Kirk talked about driving, and movies they liked, and work, and Maya had told him all about her family, Caitlin, and the gang at school. Oddly, though, she knew absolutely nothing about his family. When she had asked, he had been evasive.

"Do you have brothers and sisters?" she had asked him, on Tuesday.

"Well, I have an older sister, but she moved away years ago. I don't really know her very well," he had answered.

"What about your parents, what do they do?"

"Oh, my mom's in an office, my dad works shifts, you know, just ordinary jobs," said Kirk.

"What kind of work?" Maya had pressed.

"Ordinary stuff. I don't know that much about it," he said. "Anyway," he changed the subject, "we get paid this week."

Maya was puzzled by his reticence, but allowed herself to be diverted. "Great! Finally, I can start saving toward the van conversion."

That same afternoon, during the lull, Kirk showed Maya how to run the milkshake machine while Sarah Anne handled the customers.

"It's quite easy, really," Kirk explained. "You start with a scoop of ice-cream, and put it in the metal cup." Kirk scooped a scoop into the cup. "Then, add the milkshake stuff and the flavour from here," he went on, lifting a lever that delivered milkshake mix into the steel cup, and pumping chocolate sauce in to the mixture. "Then put it on the platform with the stirrer in it, flip this switch — " he flipped the switch, "and presto!" he finished, "milkshake happens!"

When the machine had stopped whirring, Maya reached out for the cup, and at the same moment, so did Kirk. Their fingers touched on the cold metal, but neither drew their hands away immediately. After a moment, Kirk let go, and looked down, almost embarrassed, Maya thought. She quickly took a paper cup, and poured the milkshake into it.

"Caitlin, I feel like there might be some hope with Kirk." The girls were in Maya's room listening to the radio, Maya stretched out on her side, on the bed, Caitlin flopped in a pile of cushions in the corner.

Maya's bedroom was romantic, but not frilly — actually, exotic might have been a better way of putting it. The bed, covered in an Indian-print cotton bedspread, was along one wall, under the window. In the opposite corner was the pile of cushions, covered in a variety of flowered designs, from lush South Pacific batiks, to delicate Laura Ashley prints, to English-garden chintz to stylized Guatemalan weaving, all in shades of purples, blues and greens. A thirties-style dark wood vanity on the same opposite wall had a huge oval mirror, and doubled as a desk and chest of drawers. It suited Maya's wheelchair, as she could wheel with her knees under the top of it, and the drawers were low enough for her to reach everything. On the walls, Maya had had her mom help her pin up a beautiful Afghani scarf, a Robert Doisneau poster of a couple kissing in the street, a travel poster for Israel, and a poster from *Gone With the Wind*, where Clark Gable was carrying Vivien Leigh up the staircase at Tara. The window above the bed was covered by a folding blind, with more fabric draped around the window frame. A small collection of elephants paraded across the windowsill. A wooden bookcase held all her favourite books from childhood and now, and on top was a picture of her parents on their wedding day, her mother's hair long and straight and parted in the middle, and she was wearing a voluminous muslin gown. Her father had his dark hair in an Afro, and he was wearing jeans and an Indian cotton shirt. They sort of looked funny, but Maya thought they were also kind of romantic and sweet.

"Hope with Kirk? Tell me," said Caitlin.

"Well, he takes his lunch at the same time as I do, and we always talk — and *he* got to set up the lunch schedule. And — I don't know, it's sort of hard to explain." Maya thought about the things that had been happening. The way he blushed when Scotty made that "under the hood" remark. The way he'd smile at her if he caught her eye when she was putting in an order. Or how, like at the milkshake machine, they'd find themselves touching each other. Maya knew that a lot of the time she probably initiated it, even though she didn't intend to. But she was pretty sure Kirk was the one who touched her first, a lot of the time. It was never anything significant, just that no one pulled away, and it kept happening. She tried to explain it to Caitlin.

Caitlin smiled. "I know what you mean."

"But I don't know, it's probably just wishful thinking," Maya shook her head.

"Well, it *does* sound like — maybe ... "

But Maya didn't want to get her hopes up too high. "Enough about me," she said, pulling herself up to a sitting position on the bed. "What about David?"

"We-ell," started Caitlin. "We went out again last night — do you realize that's the third time? Friday, Monday after work, and last night." Maya nodded, and Caitlin went on. "I don't know, I might be falling in love. He's so ... passionate ... it just kind of carries me along."

"Passionate?" asked Maya, knowingly. "Did he kiss you?"

Caitlin hesitated. "Oh, Maya, I think maybe he'll think I'm easy. He — um ... " Caitlin paused again. "Maya, I let him feel me up."

In spite of herself, Maya was shocked. She knew she didn't have much experience with guys, but it did seem a little fast to her, on just the third date. Although she loved the *idea* of someone touching her breasts, she thought she'd actually be kind of nervous about it, if it ever happened.

"Over or under the clothes?" asked Maya,

enthralled and aghast at the same time. Did she really want to know this?

"Oh, over, over," said Caitlin, emphatically, and then she added suddenly, "basically."

"Basically?" asked Maya.

"Well, between the clothes, if you know what I mean," confessed Caitlin. "I mean, I was wearing a bra, and that part was just at the end. I didn't let him go any farther. Though I think maybe I'd like to — later. I really, really like him."

Maya sighed. Somehow, Kirk touching her fingers at the milkshake machine didn't seem as exciting any more. "How are your driving lessons going?" she asked Caitlin.

"Not bad."

Thursday afternoon, paycheques were handed out. Maya was disappointed to see how much money was taken off for taxes and unemployment insurance and Canada Pension. Even though she knew she would probably get most or all of it back in the spring at tax time, she needed the money now. Now that she was working, she was no longer getting an allowance, of course, so some of that money had to go toward ordinary expenses. It didn't leave much to put into her driving account.

At the end of her shift, Maya wheeled back into the employees' lounge to change. She took her purse from the locker in the lounge that had been assigned to her, and took her little gold Star of David out of the side pocket. She didn't like to wear the Star at work, in case it got caught on something, or she lost it, but she had forgotten to take it off this morning when she left the house, so she had slipped it into her purse for safekeeping.

She wheeled into the washroom off the lounge, and clipped the fine chain around her neck. She pulled off her visor, and hung it around a coat hanger, and then unbuttoned her tunic, shook it out, and put it on the hanger as well, wheeling over to the coat rack to hang it up. From her bag, she pulled out a peach-coloured t-shirt, that set off her tan, and looked great with the ivory capri pants she was already wearing. She thought she heard a sound, and turned to look, but there was no one there. Turning back to the mirror, she bunched up the t-shirt, and pulled it over her head. As her head popped through the v-neck of the t-shirt, she thought she caught a glimpse of something in the mirror, but when she turned, again, there was nothing there. Still, she felt funny, almost as though someone were watching her. Don't be silly, Maya, she told herself.

You've been watching too many late movies. Maya released her hair from the ponytail she wore it in for work, shook it out, checked her reflection one more time, and set off down the corridor. As she passed Scotty's door, he called out to her, and she reversed to stop in the doorway.

"Did you call me?" she asked.

"Yes, just wanted to check that you got your paycheque all right," he answered from behind his desk.

"Oh, yes, thanks."

"Don't spend it all in one place," he said.

Maya smiled. "No, I'm putting it in the bank. I'm saving up to get my parents' van converted, so I can learn to drive," she explained.

"Oh, I thought you'd go out and spend it on nice clothes," said Scotty.

Not knowing what to say, Maya just smiled.

Scotty went on, "Maybe some lacy underthings, hm? Something peachy?"

Lacy? Peachy? Maya was wearing a peach-coloured lace bra. Scotty's millionwatt grin suddenly reminded her of the picture of the big, bad wolf in her Three Little Pigs book from when she was little, and it gave Maya the creeps. She *had* thought someone had been watching her. Had it been Scotty? The thought curdled her stomach. She managed to make a polite getaway, then zipped down the hallway and out through the front of the restaurant, her thoughts whirling around inside her.

There was a pretty, if tiny, park on the corner, about a half a block from Slurps. Maya stopped here, and took refuge under a tree, almost out of breath, trying to look like she was just enjoying the beautiful day. She had to think, she had to get her thoughts straight. Emotions tumbled around in her like socks in a washing machine. *Had* he been watching her? She was pretty sure he had. No, she *knew* he had. There was just something in his manner toward her, a familiarity on his part that made her feel like she'd been spied on. And to think that only last night, she'd been wondering what it might be like to have someone touch her breasts. She couldn't even cope with having someone *see* them, even with a bra on. She felt used and dirty, and she hadn't even done anything. She tried to brush the ugly image of Scotty and his wolf-teeth from her mind, but his leering face kept surfacing, even when she closed her eyes.

"Maya!" Oh, God, he's followed me. She looked up startled. And then, she relaxed. It was Kirk, leaning out a car window. "Maya! What are you doing? Do you want a ride?"

Maya suddenly realized she just didn't want to be alone. She nodded, and wheeled over towards the car. Kirk hopped out and opened the front door. He offered Maya his hand, but she pushed herself up out of the chair, and, holding the car door, transferred into the passenger seat. As she pulled the door closed behind her, Kirk pushed the wheelchair to the back of the car, opened the trunk and lifted it in, lowering the trunk lid as far as it would go. In a moment, he was beside her, behind the wheel.

"Well, where to?" he asked, cheerfully.

Maya looked at him blankly.

"Where do you live?" asked Kirk.

"Um ... oh!, um, up by Degrassi High. Just up and to the right at the lights," Maya said, pulling herself out of her daze.

But Kirk didn't put the car in gear. Instead, he looked at her closely. "Are you okay?" he asked "Something wrong?"

"No, no," said Maya, airily. "Just lost in thought — uh — I was figuring out how soon it would be before I could start my driving lessons," she lied.

"And?" Kirk replied.

"And what?" asked Maya.

"How long before you can start your driving lessons?"

"Oh — uh — I hadn't quite worked it out. I'm hopeless at mental arithmetic," she laughed. This, at least, was true.

"Do you have to go home right away?" Kirk was asking her. "You could come over and see my car, if you want to."

Scotty's face in Maya's thoughts popped like a soap bubble and was gone. Go over to Kirk's place? Oh yes!

"That would be nice," she replied, casually. "So this isn't your car?"

"No, it's my dad's," explained Kirk. "I was running late this morning. This car's not much, either, I admit," he went on, "but it runs, which is more than you can say for mine."

The car *was* a bit grungy, a dirty green, big, old car, Maya thought an American one, but she wasn't much good at things like that. The interior could have done with a good cleaning. There were sty-rofoam cups, an empty Burger King bag, a very ratty grocery store bag, parking receipts, a broken ice-scraper and a lot of grit on the floor. A spring was prodding Maya's back, and the upholstery was somewhat worn in areas. As Kirk shifted into drive, Maya reached for her seatbelt, but couldn't find one.

"Oh, sorry, half of that seatbelt is missing," said Kirk. "Don't worry, I won't let you get killed."

Maya laughed nervously. Chances were that she wouldn't get killed, but not having the seatbelt made her edgy.

The drive to Kirk's took about five minutes. Kirk lived in a part of town that, though she'd driven through it often, she really didn't know well. His house actually wasn't far from Melanie's place, but Maya had never been to Melanie's, because she couldn't get up the iron staircase to Melanie's apartment.

Kirk pulled the car into a parking spot behind his house, next to a big beige car. He got out Maya's chair, and brought it round for her to get into, then led the way through the gate into the back yard.

"Wait here," he instructed her. "My dad's on weird shifts, so he's probably asleep. I don't want to disturb him. I'll just get us a Coke. Is Coke okay?"

"Fine," said Maya. She felt a little disappointed that they weren't going to go into his house. She wanted to know more about him. Besides that, there were a few stairs up. It would have been nice to have Kirk carry her up the stairs, like Clark Gable and Vivien Leigh in *Gone With the Wind*. As she sat on the patio waiting, she looked around the yard. Someone had once loved it — there was the weedy ruin of a vegetable garden, rusty tomato cages at odd angles still stuck in the ground. A honeysuckle bush had grown wild, strangling several other bushes, but filling the air with its sweet fragrance. The lawn was weedy, but it was mowed, and grass and some rather pretty purple flowers grew up between the paving stones of the patio.

The house itself was two stories high. It looked like it was made of brick, but it was really some type of covering that looked like brick, peeling away in a few areas. The concrete back porch looked sturdy, but paint was flaking off the iron railings. All the windows were covered with closed rolling blinds, which just made Maya even more curious about what it was like inside.

# Chapter 6

Looking at the windows, Maya thought she heard muffled voices inside the house. Maybe Kirk's dad was up, and she'd get invited inside. Maya assumed his mother was at work, if she worked in an office.

But in a moment, Kirk returned, carrying the two cans of Coke.

"He's asleep," he confirmed. Maya guessed the voices must have come from some other house. "Here," he said, offering her the can, adding, "come see the car."

They went back out through the gate, to where the beige car was parked. "There she is," Kirk announced, gesturing expansively. "Lady Godiva."

"Lady Godiva?" asked Maya.

Kirk looked a little embarrassed. "I've stripped her down to practically nothing," he explained. "But maybe when she's up and running I'll give her a new name. I've been working on the engine first," he went on. "Come see."

Maya wheeled around to the front of the car, and managed to slip into the few feet between the wooden fence and the front of the car. Kirk raised the hood, and then sat down on an upturned metal drum of some kind. As he did, he glanced at the Star of David at Maya's throat. He reached out and took it between his thumb and finger. Where he touched her skin, Maya was tingling. She held her breath. What was he doing?

"I didn't know you were Jewish," he said.

"With a name like Goldberg?" laughed Maya.

"My mother was Jewish," he said, almost to himself. He let go of the Star, and turned his attention to the car before Maya could ask him what he meant by "was."

"You see, this part, this is all new. You see, these connections, and I got this bit at the junkyard for free."

It didn't make any sense to Maya. But nothing here did. He said his mother worked in an office, but then he referred to her in the past tense. He said his father was asleep, but she was sure she had heard voices from the house. There was a lot Maya didn't know about Kirk. Should she have come here, alone, with him? No one even knew where she was! She didn't even know his last name.

" ... do you follow me?" he was saying.

Maya nodded, though he might as well have been explaining the workings of a nuclear submarine in Swahili. Kirk grinned at her.

"No you don't," he accused her.

"Well, not all the details," she admitted. "I don't even know your last name."

"Buchanan," he said, "but that doesn't affect the workings of the engine much."

"Kirk Buchanan, man of mystery," teased Maya.

Kirk looked down, then up at Maya. Maya found herself looking straight into those tender eyes. Her breath caught in her throat.

"Let's not talk about me ... " he said, leaning forward just a little. "I'm — I'm not very interesting."

"You are to me," said Maya, intending to say it jokingly, but she was surprised to find that it came out seriously. The angles of the fence and the open car hood created a small, private universe for them. Maya could smell metal and oil. A squirrel scolded them nearby. Kirk's lips tasted sweet, like pink lemonade. A chaste kiss. Maya's eyes fluttered open, but she saw that Kirk's were still closed, and she kissed him again. More.

Maya relived the next few minutes over and over again in bed that night. No longer was she sweet sixteen and never been kissed. Kirk had driven her home in time for supper — her dad was making hamburgers on the grill, the last thing she wanted after a day at Slurps. Her mother was a little irritated that she hadn't called to say where she was. Bubbie asked her, very seriously, if he was a nice boy, and told her not to let boys take advantage of her. But Maya did not feel taken advantage of. She felt starry-eyed, swept off her feet, head in the clouds, glowing. Why was it that something that felt as good as this made her descend to mere clichés when she tried to describe it? She had even tried to write a poem this evening — that in itself was a bit of a cliché — but all she could come up with was drivel.

Maya lay in bed, clasping the pillow to her. It felt nothing like Kirk, but at least it had substance. Never again would daydreams be enough. There was nothing like the real thing. Oh, gross, Maya, now it's commercials as well as clichés. Maya went over the afternoon, stroking it and turning it in her mind like a cherished object. When she kissed him the second time, she had thought, now I've been kissed twice. But now she didn't know how many times she'd been kissed — somehow counting seemed wrong, if it had even been possible to focus on something like numbers. She ran her hand across her cheek, like he had. And in the car when they got home, he held her so close. She wished he were there to kiss again, there was nothing in her imagination that could make her really feel that kiss. She felt like she was floating on a sea of emotion (not more clichés, Maya!). With one arm around her pillow, the other hand touching her cheek, she drifted off to sleep, hoping she would dream about Kirk.

Maya was curled in Kirk's arms. They were floating on an air mattress for two in a quiet lagoon where orchids or some sort of exotic flowers were floating in the water. Maya picked one and, as she handed it to Kirk, he leaned over and kissed her, pulling her close to him, and she melted into his arms. Gradually, it started to get darker, and when Maya reached out, she found that the water had become chilly. Kirk pulled away, saying, "What's the definition of a mistress? Half-way between a mister and a mattress! Ha ha! I'll huff and I'll puff and I'll *blow* your clothes off!" Suddenly, Maya was naked and shivering, and when she looked up, she saw, not Kirk, but a wolf wearing a navy blue suit. Then they were no longer in a lagoon, but some sort of house, and Maya was looking down from a landing. The wolf was carrying a baby girl up a curving staircase, licking her throat and testing her skin with his teeth. Maya could see a little Star of David on a chain around the baby's neck. Maya wheeled her chair to the edge of the landing to rescue the baby, but could get no closer to them, as steps seemed to be adding themselves to the staircase as the wolf climbed up. The wolf opened its mouth, and Maya was sure he was going to eat the baby. "No!" yelled Maya, and suddenly she found herself in her bedroom, awake, staring at the poster of Clark Gable and Vivien Leigh. She pulled herself into a sitting position so she wouldn't fall back asleep and slide back into the dream. Her sheets were tossed back, and her pillow was on the floor. Maya pulled them up around herself, huddling up tight until she stopped shaking.

Maya needn't have worried about slipping back into the dream. Even after she calmed down, she continued to lie awake. She tried to think about Kirk, about kissing him, to recapture the sensations, but she kept seeing Scotty and his toothy smile. It didn't make sense. She should be flattered to have so many people interested in her. But that was just it — it didn't seem like Scotty was interested in *her*, just in her body. While Kirk was more of a friend. Was it just that she wasn't attracted to Scotty? Was what he was doing so very bad? She had heard that guys would take any opportunity to get what they could from females. That was all Scotty was doing. Right? Was that all Kirk was doing? Still, it felt different. Was that only because she wanted Kirk's attention, and not Scotty's? But was that so wrong, even if it were true? Maybe she could find a way of saying something to Scotty, to make him back off. But what? "Gee, Scotty, I really wish you wouldn't spy on me when I'm getting changed"? That sounded really conversational. He'd tell her she was nuts. Maybe she should just quit, maybe her parents were right in the first place, she shouldn't have a job. But maybe it wouldn't happen again. Or maybe, just maybe, Scotty wasn't really doing anything, maybe it was her imagination. She obviously had a lethal imagination, if she could get the big, bad wolf and Clark Gable together in a navy blue suit at Tara. But she couldn't quite convince herself. The sense of being watched was too strong, his comment about a peach lace bra too accurate to be coincidence. Maybe he would do it again. Maybe worse. But if she quit, she'd lose the chance to make all that money, and she hadn't earned much yet. And she wouldn't see Kirk any more. Why was life so complicated? Oh, well, tomorrow, was her day off, and in the evening, Caitlin was coming over. She didn't have to make a decision right now. Maybe Caitlin would have some good advice. The black velvet sky was washing to a smoky grey and the stars were slowly disappearing as exhaustion finally carried Maya off to sleep.

Since it was her day off, Maya slept in the next morning, and awoke to find she had the house to herself. There was a note on the kitchen counter that said, "We have all gone to the zoo — thought you'd rather sleep in. See you at dinner time. Love, M, B, J & J."

Maya popped a waffle in the toaster — a treat that was supposed to be reserved for Sundays — and indulged herself in the morning TV talk shows. She had secretly hoped one of them would be about "Bosses that Spy on their Semi-Nude Employees" or "Girls Who Kiss Boys Whose Last Names They've Only Just Found Out," or maybe "Weird Dreams and What They Mean: An Expert Interprets — Call Our Toll-Free Number." But it was only the standard stuff — "Housewives Who Work as Call-Girls" on one channel, and

"Women Who Refuse to Take Off Their Wedding Gowns" on the other.

She thought about the Scotty situation. In the light of day, it didn't seem so bad — what was it that Bubbie always said? "Even a spotted pig looks black at night." Probably she had imagined the whole thing about him spying on her — it was just a lucky guess with the peachy-lacy remark. Yeah, that must be it. Sure, he was an old-lech-in-training, but Maya could handle it. Anyway, given how hard it had been to get the job in the first place, she'd be crazy to quit now. She'd never get another job at this point in the summer, not with zero experience, a wheelchair, and a record of quitting. And most of all, there'd be no Kirk. And so Maya decided to pretend nothing happened, even though she knew, somewhere deep down, that it really had.

She decided instead to think about Kirk, smiling at the memory their first kiss, and switched to MuchMusic as she poured a little extra maple syrup on her waffle.

# Chapter 7

As Maya finished loading the dishwasher after dinner, Caitlin arrived. The girls settled themselves on the front porch, and for Maya, it wasn't a moment too soon. The music videos had worn thin, and Maya had spent part of the day reading, and part budgeting her earnings, which was actually sort of fun. Having the day off to think about the Scotty situation had been kind of a mixed blessing — she hadn't really wanted to think about Scotty at all, and it kept her away from Kirk. And she had been dying all day to talk to Caitlin.

Caitlin, however, was full of her own news. Maya decided to keep her excitement to herself, and spring it on Caitlin when she was least expecting it.

After checking to make sure that all of Maya's family was safely out of earshot, the girls spoke in low voices.

"Maya, do you think it's okay to have sex if you're not married?"

"You didn't!" exclaimed Maya, in a combination of a whisper and a scream.

"No, no, no," said Caitlin quickly. "I just — what do you think?"

"I think, if you love the person, it might be okay, as long as it's safe sex and you don't get pregnant. It sort of depends," was Maya's reply.

"That's what I think, too," said Caitlin. "I think I love him, Maya. How can you tell if it's love?"

Until yesterday, Maya would have sarcastically said to herself, How would I know? But today, she was starting to understand what Caitlin meant. She had felt "in love" with Kirk ever since she had met him, but she knew you couldn't really call it anything but infatuation if there was no real relationship there. But now that he had kissed her, and she felt like a bubble, like a star, like a glass of ginger ale inside, she realized that you couldn't tell, not for sure. And was there a difference between "love" and "in love"? And did "in love" count, if you were thinking of having sex?

"I always thought you were just supposed to know when it happened," Maya finally answered, not at all sure that was true.

"Then I guess maybe I am," sighed Caitlin. "I mean, things are progressing fast. I mean — what would you say second base was?"

"Second base? Maybe — under the clothes?"

"Well — second base," said Caitlin.

Maya wasn't surprised. She hadn't got to first base yet, if it was over the clothes, but she could sort of see how it would happen.

"So." Caitlin looked over at Maya. "How's Kirk? Any progress?"

Maya tried to look casual and straight-faced, but her face broke into a grin in spite of itself. "Progress," she announced.

Caitlin squealed. "Tell me. Tell me everything."

"Well ... " Where should she start? Not with Scotty. She decided not to say anything about Scotty at all. She had no real evidence, she was probably just imagining it. "I was on my way home from work, and he offered me a ride. Then, we went to his place, and I had a Coke ... and ... he kissed me!"

"Maya, that's great!"

"I know," said Maya, grinning her head off.

"Where does he live? What's his house like?" asked Caitlin.

"He lives down near Melanie. His house is ... ordinary. I don't think he's too rich. We didn't go inside." Maya paused, unsure if she should tell Caitlin about her concerns,

71

and decided to plunge on. "It's sort of weird, though. We didn't go in, because he said his dad was sleeping, but I was sure I heard voices inside the house. And he told me before his mom works in an office, but then he said, 'My mother was Jewish.' Was. Don't you think that's odd?"

"Maybe she used to be Jewish, and now she's not. Maybe she converted or something," suggested Caitlin.

"No, not the way he said it. The 'was' meant his mother, not the Jewish part."

"Maybe the one who works in an office is his stepmother. Maybe his real mother died."

That made sense. That would explain why he seemed wistful about it, too. "That's probably it," agreed Maya. "But what about the voices?"

"Maybe his dad woke up when Kirk went in," suggested Caitlin.

"No, because he said 'He's asleep' when he came back out."

"Maybe it was the radio, or the TV," said Caitlin. "And Kirk turned it off, which is why you didn't hear it when he came out."

"There're all kinds of explanations. But he didn't want me in the house. I could just tell," said Maya. "Caitlin, did I tell you what gorgeous eyes he has?"

As she buzzed along the sidewalk to work the next morning, Maya started to get nervous. She hadn't seen Kirk for a whole day. Maybe he'd changed his mind, maybe it was just a fluke that he'd kissed her. She'd heard about that sort of thing happening — a couple making out at a party, and then the next day, the guy wouldn't talk to the girl. And then there was Scotty. She hoped that situation was over and done with. She hadn't felt this nervous since coming to work her first day. Taking a deep breath, she pushed open the door to Slurps and rolled in.

Everything looked exactly the same as normal. Sarah Anne was pushing napkins into the dispensers. In the kitchen, she could make out Grace and Kei-Kei and Tommy and Shazia chopping condiments — well, the last three were watching a cheerleading routine Grace was demonstrating. Kirk came out of the back, adjusting his two-pointed cap, and watching Grace with amusement.

"Morning, everybody," he said, with a grin, looking around, and finishing on Maya. And he added a little something extra to his grin, just for her. No one else would have noticed, but she did, and she knew it was okay. She smiled back.

Maya went into the back room and changed as quickly as she could. As she wheeled past Scotty's office, he called out to her, just as he had on Thursday. She stopped in the doorway.

"Come in, come in," he beckoned.

Maya rolled a little farther in, thinking of the spider and the fly. Scotty crossed behind her and closed the door. Maya's stomach flopped over. But he wouldn't try anything, would he? Not with everyone around. Scotty obviously noticed her discomfort, because he put his hand on her shoulder. Maya nearly recoiled, but just managed to stay her ground.

"Don't be nervous," said Scotty, in what Maya assumed was supposed to be a reassuring voice, but sounded creepy to her. "I just wanted to tell you how well I think you're doing."

Maya was surprised. She knew she'd caught on quickly, but she didn't think she was doing anything special.

"You've been here a few weeks now, and I don't really think minimum wage is enough. I know how keen you are to start your driving lessons, so I'd like to give you a little raise. Twenty-five cents an hour." He smiled, all his teeth in an even line. All the better to eat you with, my dear.

"Thank you," Maya said, completely taken aback. Why was Scotty giving her a raise?

"Now, we don't like our employees to talk about their salaries to each other. We'll just keep this between us, shall we? I know you're not the blabbing type." He smiled again.

So that was it. Hush money. Scotty was paying her not to say anything about his spying on her the other day. Which meant she was right, he was spying. Never mind, Maya. Don't look a gift horse in the mouth, they always say. And money was money. After all, she *was* doing a good job, and minimum wage really was ridiculously low. Even without much of a head for math, Maya knew it meant an extra ten dollars a week, and that was nothing to sneeze at.

"Thank you," said Maya quietly. "I'd better get out front, now."

Even though Maya had justified the raise in her mind, it kept popping up to bother her all morning long. She didn't like the idea of being bribed to keep quiet, but she reminded herself she hadn't planned to say anything to anyone anyway.

At lunch, Kirk joined Maya at the picnic table outside.

"Missed you yesterday," he said, as he climbed over the bench and sat down.

Yes! This was exactly what Maya wanted to hear. "Me, too," she said, hoping that what felt like a rush of blood to her face was actually turning her a delicate shade of pink. At least Kirk was looking down.

"Um, I was wondering ... " he went on. He seemed tense.

A date! He was going to ask her out on a date! Here she had kissed him, and she hadn't even been on a date with him — kissing *before* the first date. Or was that an old-fashioned thing? It seemed like it must be. Caitlin didn't seem to have any problem with it. "Mm-hm ... ?" she encouraged him.

"What — uh — did Scotty want this morning?"

Oh, great. Not only wasn't it a date, what was she going to say when Scotty had just asked her not to say anything? It wasn't like she had any great loyalty to Scotty, but she didn't want to get into it herself. She definitely didn't want to reveal her suspicion that Scotty had been spying on her. "Um, nothing, really," she lied, concentrating on her french fries, so Kirk couldn't see her eyes. She hated lying to Kirk. "He just wanted to say that he was pleased with the work I was doing."

Kirk seemed to suddenly relax, which was kind of odd. "Good," he said, then he smiled. "I mean, that's good that he's pleased with your work."

"Yes, I guess it is," said Maya, and then she quickly changed the subject to something more ordinary.

When Maya got changed to go home that night, again, she did it as quickly as she could, this time facing the door. Yet she still felt creepy, as though she were being watched. Was it just because of the other day, or could Scotty see her from somewhere? His office backed on to the washroom, but she'd been in there, and she hadn't seen any trap doors or periscopes or anything. Could there be a gap in the paneling that he looked through? She glanced along the wall in the washroom, but she didn't see anything unusual. The horrible thought occurred to her that not only was her raise to keep her quiet, but that maybe he somehow thought he had paid her to let him watch her. It made her feel absolutely creepy.

The next day, the weather was overcast and damp, so Maya decided to wear a long-sleeved top under her uniform. When she realized that she didn't have to take it off to get changed into or out of her uniform, she knew that she had found the solution to her problem.

The third day that she wore the long-sleeved top, even though the weather was nice again, Scotty stopped her in the hall.

"Cold?" he asked her.

"No, why?" said Maya.

"I notice you've been wearing long sleeves. I wondered if the air conditioning was too cold for you."

Maya eyed Scotty. He probably knew nothing about her, really, nothing about spina bifida or wheelchairs or anything. She decided to risk it. "I just have to be careful with my health," she explained. "Spina bifida affects the lungs, you know. I have to be careful in air conditioning — too easy to catch colds." What a lot of lying she was doing these days.

"I'll take it down a notch or two, though," said Scotty. "I always forget that not everyone is in a suit jacket like me. I'd rather have everyone wearing the same uniform — looks neater." He smiled and went over to the thermostat as Maya continued down the hall.

So it was a game, now, thought Maya. Well, that meant two could play. The next day, Maya wore a tank top to work, and put her uniform over top. How could Scotty say anything about that? If he commented that she was wearing the tank top, it would reveal that he was looking for sure, because there was no other way he could know what she had on under her tunic. And what objection could he possibly raise?

# Chapter 8

The tank top seemed to do the trick, and Maya managed to keep away from Scotty most of the time. Life, in fact, was pretty good. Her bank account was building up — soon she'd have enough money for the van conversion, and then maybe she'd be able to persuade her parents to let her start driving lessons. And Kirk — that was like living in a wonderful dream.

They still talked during the lunch hours, and they never ran out of things to talk about. They'd tell each other about funny things that had happened to them in school, or talk about their favourite movies. Caitlin was pretty busy with David these days, so it was extra nice that sometimes they'd go out for coffee after work — just casual, not like a date, exactly — and then they'd talk about more important things, what they dreamed of, the future.

"Lady Godiva is coming along," he told

her one day, as they sat in The Donut Shoppe, after work, sipping on Cokes. "I worked on the exhaust system all weekend, and I think I won't asphyxiate myself somewhere on the road between Thunder Bay and Winnipeg."

"Winnipeg?" asked Maya.

"Just after Labour Day, Lady Godiva should be finished. I'm gone."

"Gone? To Winnipeg? Why?" This was all news to Maya. He was leaving her?

"Not Winnipeg," he said. "Probably B.C., maybe on the coast somewhere, or maybe Alberta. It depends."

"For a vacation?" asked Maya, hoping, but not hopeful.

Kirk smiled. "Not a vacation. Forever. Freedom, like I told you before."

"But —" This wasn't fair, this couldn't be happening! "Freedom from what? Won't you miss ... home?" She wanted to say, Won't you miss me? but she stopped herself.

"Home!" snorted Kirk, then he shook his head sadly. "No." He raised his head, and went on in a firm voice. "I won't miss that place."

"Your mom and dad?" asked Maya quietly.

"Oh, I don't see that much of them anyway," he said, dismissively. "My mom's pretty busy, and my dad's on shifts — you know."

Maya took a sip from her Coke. As much as it seemed unfair that he was leaving her, her romantic soul could see the appeal. She could envision him driving Lady Godiva across snow-covered fields of wheat stubble, the wind in his hair, the radio cranked up (okay, if there was snow, he probably wouldn't have the window open, but the picture was better that way). Or stopping for gas along the north shore of Superior, some native guy in a checked jacket pumping gas, country music wailing from the radio in the store where Kirk was buying a sandwich. Checking into a cheap motel in Alberta, called The Driver's Rest, except half the neon would be burned out, and the sign would just say "The D ive." Then through the breathtaking Rockies, and the treed hills on the other side, then over more mountains and to the sea sparkling below. Maya had made the trip with her family years before, before Joel was even born. To do it on your own, in Lady Godiva … Maya wished there were some way she could go too, but she knew it was impossible.

When she told him about what she imagined — except the part about going with him — he laughed. "That's what's so great about you," he said. "You've got the wildest imagination. I'm wondering if I'm crazy to think I can do it, and you're making some fleabag motel sound romantic."

Sometimes, though not very often, they would go to Kirk's place, and there they wouldn't talk so much, but would end up making out in the car that didn't yet run.

One day, when they were at his place, he did ask her about her wheelchair.

"You know, it amazes me how you get around in that thing," he commented, when they were in the back, looking at the latest developments on Lady Godiva. "I think if I asked you to move over one inch, you could. Most people don't drive *cars* so well."

Maya smiled, and zigzagged one inch to her left. "Most people don't spend all their waking hours in cars," Maya pointed out. "You could move over one inch too, if I asked you."

"Yeah," agreed Kirk, "but humans are a lot more complicated than the machines they can design."

"Want to try it?" Maya asked him suddenly.

He looked at her in surprise, and glanced at his house. "Sure," he said. "If you don't mind."

"Not at all."

Kirk carried the metal drum he had been sitting on down to the lane, and Maya transferred to it to watch him while he positioned himself in the chair.

"The footrests are probably a little high for you," Maya commented, "but it won't make any difference for trying it out. Just press the lever."

Kirk pushed the lever on the armrest, and the chair shot forward, stopping abruptly when he let go of the lever.

"Gently," said Maya.

Kirk tried again, and soon he was buzzing along the lane, grinning from ear to ear. He tried backing up, and swung in a circle. "This is cool," he exclaimed. "It's like the joystick on a video game, except you really move."

"Now go through the gate," instructed Maya.

Kirk zipped the chair alongside his father's car, up to the gate into his back yard, which opened toward him. Stopping, he unlatched the gate, then found he couldn't open it, as he was in his own way. He zigzagged jerkily to the left, and reached to open the gate. Maya was grinning quietly to herself. It wasn't fair, really, because after all, she had been using the chair every day for years, but she could never help but be amused when an able-bodied person tried it. By now Kirk was through the gate.

"Now close it behind you!" Maya exclaimed.

Kirk turned and looked balefully at her.

Obviously, he couldn't reach it from where he was now. He stood up, strode to the gate and closed it.

"Happy now?" he said grimly. "I'm holding your chair hostage until you wipe that smirk off your face."

The two collapsed in laughter.

Maya had tried to get Kirk to come for dinner, but he wouldn't, although he had at least met all of her family. One day he had given her a ride home after being at The Donut Shoppe, and as he was unloading her wheelchair from the trunk, Bubbie had come out, and invited him to come in.

"Oh, no, I'd better be getting back," Kirk had said.

"Oh, come on," said Maya. "My family doesn't bite. I'd like you to meet them. Stay for supper."

"No, I can't stay for supper. I promised my dad I'd cook tonight."

"Well, at least come in and meet them."

So Kirk locked up his dad's car, and came up the walk.

"Bubbie, this is Kirk, Kirk this is my grandmother, Mrs. Levy," Maya introduced the two.

"Hello, Kirk," said Bubbie warmly, "Come in, come in." She put her arm around him, and led him into the house. "Karen, here's Maya's friend Kirk," she called into the kitchen where Mrs. Goldberg was washing vegetables. Kirk glanced over his shoulder at Maya and the two exchanged a grin.

Janna and Joel appeared from nowhere, and Joel stared at Kirk, who was nearly twice his height. Maya introduced them, and Mrs. Goldberg came out from the kitchen, wiping her hands on a tea towel.

"Hello, Kirk, will you stay to dinner?" asked Maya's mom, shaking Kirk's hand.

"That's very nice of you Mrs. Goldberg," said Kirk, "but really, I have to go."

Just then, Mr. Goldberg arrived home, and he, too, invited Kirk to stay.

"I'm making my famous Lemon Grilled Chicken," he offered. But Kirk was adamant, and soon he was gone.

At dinner, everyone passed judgement on him. "He's really tall," said Joel, in a voice tinged with awe.

"Maya's got a boyfriend, Maya's got a boyfriend," said Janna, in a sing-song voice.

Maya brandished a forkful of Lemon Grilled Chicken at her sister. "Janna, you keep that up, and you'll get this, fork and all, down your throat."

"Maya," cautioned her mother. "I thought he seemed very polite," she went on.

"Good-looking, too," sparkled Bubbie.

"Nice to see you making new friends," said her Dad.

That evening, Bubbie popped in to Maya's bedroom. Maya was writing a poem about suicide. It was weird, how, when she was happy, she could write great stuff about misery, but when she was miserable, all that came out was chirpy little verses.

"Come in," she invited Bubbie, closing her notebook, so Bubbie wouldn't see what she was writing.

Bubbie sat on the bed.

"He's a nice boy, this Kirk?" asked Bubbie.

"Yes," said Maya. She knew what Bubbie meant — was he trying to take advantage of her, or did he treat her like a lady?

"Not Jewish?" Bubbie asked.

"Actually, his mother's Jewish," responded Maya. "So I guess that makes him Jewish."

"Not raised Jewish," Bubbie pressed on.

"Bubbie, I'm not marrying him," said Maya.

"You never know which is the one you're going to marry," answered Bubbie. "I met your Zaide when I was only seventeen. But, I know, you're still young. Just be careful. I'm sure you wonder sometimes where you're going to find a man who can see past your wheelchair and love you. I think it's nice this boy likes you, but there'll be lots more, you know. Be patient."

"I know, Bubbie." Maya knew she was cautioning her against having sex too fast. As if that were likely. But it was nice that her grandmother took the trouble. "Give me a hug, Bubbie," she said, stretching out her arms. "I love you."

"I love you too, my *shayna maidl.*" Bubbie's eyes were glistening as she reached out and pulled Maya close to her.

After that, Kirk occasionally came over, though never for dinner. They had even made out at Maya's house once, in a quiet corner of the back yard when the others were inside, but it hadn't been much fun, because Maya was sure Joel would come screaming around, convinced he was an airplane or something, and spoil it. Or worse, Janna would discover them, and she'd never hear the end of it.

And at work, Kirk treated Maya just the same as he treated everyone else — always friendly, sometimes with a little extra smile for her that no one else would see.

No one would ever have guessed there was anything going on between Kirk and Maya, and once, when Sarah Anne made a comment about her always having so much to talk about on lunch with Kirk, Maya just laughed it off. She sensed that Kirk wanted to keep it private, and somehow, Maya kind of wanted to keep it to herself, too. She liked that she knew more about "Señor Mysterioso" than the others. She liked being the only one who knew his favourite colour (black), his favourite food (fried calamari), and his favourite movie (it had taken her a while to get it out of him — *It's a Wonderful Life*). She was afraid that if the others knew, they would tease them, and Kirk might turn away from her.

Maya was talking to Caitlin on the phone.

"Come over tomorrow," she said. "I haven't seen you in ages. What's been happening?"

"Why don't you come for dinner here?" invited Caitlin. "My mom's been saying she hasn't seen you in way too long. I think she means I'm spending too much time with David."

"I'd love to," Maya replied to the invitation. "What time?"

"How about six-thirty? Guess what, I'm doing my driving test tomorrow — it'll be a celebration!"

"Great!" was Maya's reply. Caitlin must have noticed the envious note in her voice.

"Don't worry, you'll get your license soon," said Caitlin. "And in the meantime, at least I can take us wherever we want to go. Assuming my mom and dad let me take the car."

When Maya arrived, Caitlin had not yet returned from her driving test, but Mrs. Ryan helped Maya up the three stairs on the front porch and hauled up her wheelchair. Maya had come in her manual chair just to make this easier, and also because it wasn't too far.

"There's some corn chips and salsa on the coffee table, just help yourself," said Mrs. Ryan. "I just have to stir the chili, I'll be right out."

Maya could smell the spicy scent of the chili, and dived for a chip. She was starving. She hoped Caitlin would arrive soon.

Caitlin's mother returned to the living room a moment later and they chatted for a good ten minutes before they heard Caitlin's footsteps on the porch. As soon as she opened the screen door, Maya called out to her friend.

"Let's see it, let's see the license!"

"What license?" said Caitlin, glumly. She looked as if she'd been crying.

"Didn't you pass?" asked Maya.

Caitlin's mother crossed the room and gave her daughter a hug. "Don't worry, you'll get it next time," she said.

Caitlin flopped down on the couch. "Yeah," she said, crossly. Then, after a pause, "It was so dumb. The examiner was so dumb."

Maya looked at her friend with sympathy. Even though a tiny part of her was glad to discover that Caitlin wasn't absolutely perfect, she felt for her. It wasn't easy to fail at something, especially for someone like Caitlin, who was used to instant success at everything.

Caitlin went on. "I mean, I only made two teeny mistakes and they flunked me."

"What did you do?" asked Mrs. Ryan.

"When I parallel parked, he said I was too far from the edge. I mean, did he measure it? No. And I went through a crosswalk. The person wasn't even on the crosswalk, she was standing on the curb still."

"Well, it's okay not to be perfect, that's why they have a test. You just need a little more practice, that's all," said Mrs. Ryan reassuringly. "Come on, let's eat, your dad said he'd be late. Maya must be starving."

Maya was, even if she had demolished half the corn chips.

After dinner, Mrs. Ryan went upstairs to mark summer school papers, leaving the girls alone in the living room. Caitlin hadn't really cheered up.

"Is something bothering you?" Maya asked, once they had the room to themselves.

"No, I only flunked my driving test, but nothing's bothering me," snapped Caitlin sarcastically.

"It seems like more than that," said Maya. "I mean, I'm sorry about your driving test, but you seem funny. Is it something with David?"

"Yes, it's something with David," Caitlin said, with a real anger in her voice.

"Whoa, Caitlin, this is me, don't bite my head off," said Maya. "What is it?"

"I'm sorry," Caitlin apologized, and she hugged a throw cushion to her chest, slouching low on the sofa. "It's that — things are kind of getting out of control. Last night, we went out, and he had some wine, very romantic, and — you know me, Maya, I hardly ever drink wine, maybe on Christmas. Anyway, we were supposed to go to a movie, but instead, we went down by the bluffs, and he pulled out this bottle of wine — pink, fizzy stuff, tasted like pop, only with an edge, you know? Anyway, before I knew it, I was feeling warm, and a little dizzy, and we started kissing, really hot, and — " Caitlin stopped, looking at Maya. "Third base."

"*Third* base?" asked Maya, even though

she knew she shouldn't have been surprised. "Did he — did *you* do anything?"

"A bit," admitted Caitlin. "But I managed to put the brakes on. Then he got kind of mad, and said you could hurt a guy doing that. Is that true, Maya? I mean, he meant literally hurt, not like 'I'm hurt.' Like, do damage."

"I doubt it's true," said Maya, laughing, "or there'd be a lot of damaged guys walking around."

"It's not funny, Maya. He started calling me a tease, and — well, we made up in the end, but I have the feeling that once you've reached a base, you can't go back, you know, that he's going to want to do it again. And then — home run. I'm scared he'll dump me if I say no."

"Caitlin, it's your body, not his. If he dumps you it's his loss."

"I think I love him, though. He says if I love him I would. He says it's a way to show love. I have to admit, I'm sort of curious. But then sometimes I'm not sure if I do love him."

"Then don't do it," said Maya.

"Listen, Maya, are things still going well with you and Kirk?"

Maya grinned. "Very well."

"I was wondering," said Caitlin, hesitating. "I'm a little nervous as to what might happen on our next date. I was wondering

92

if you and Kirk would like to double with us. Sort of as protection. And you can meet him, too. I'd like to meet Kirk."

Maya smiled. A date. A real date with Kirk. And going out on a double date with Caitlin and David sounded so sophisticated — it made her and Kirk a real couple. They'd never actually gone on a real date before. Maya thought it was sweet, how he could be so shy in public, and so passionate when they were alone, although things had certainly not progressed to anything like third base. But to go out on a date — that was like going public. They'd be a real couple. Maya nodded at Caitlin. "You're on."

# Chapter 9

"Where should we go?" asked Maya enthusiastically.

"How about a movie?" suggested Caitlin. "I heard *Quick Change* is supposed to be funny. I don't want to go to anything too romantic or hot, under the circumstances. It's on at the Princess."

"The Princess is accessible, so it's fine with me."

"I really want to keep things casual, so why don't we all meet there?" said Caitlin. "We can go out for pizza or something afterwards."

"Good idea. I mean about meeting there. Kirk and I haven't been on a real date yet, so if I'm asking him — it just seems more casual that way, you're right."

Maya had decided to ask Kirk out at lunch at work the next day. She felt kind of nervous about it — what if he said no?

But then, why would he say no? They were good friends, it was just a casual thing, anyway, not a *date* date, and they'd made out enough times. Of course he would say yes. But still, it made Maya a little more sympathetic to boys. Feminism or not, they seemed to still have to do most of the asking out.

As usual, Kirk joined Maya at the picnic table half-way through her lunch.

"Hi, what's happening?" he said, as he sat down.

"Hi, Kirk." Boy was she nervous. "I went over to Caitlin's last night," she said. "She flunked her driver's license."

"Too bad," said Kirk.

"Anyway, we were thinking she should go to a funny movie to cheer her up. And she said why not have you come along. And her friend David, of course."

"Um ... " said Kirk, taking a large bite out of his hamburger. He held up his finger, to signal her to wait, as he chewed the mouthful. Didn't he want to go? Was he buying time to think of an excuse? Maya was on tenterhooks. What were tenterhooks anyway? She'd have to look it up in the dictionary when she got home, she decided, but if this was tenterhooks, it was undoubtedly some form of medieval torture. "Sure, why not? Tonight?" came Kirk's reply, finally.

Thank you, Lord! Trying to act casual, like she had dates with guys all the time, she went on. "We thought we'd all just meet at the Princess, and see *Quick Change*. Caitlin says she heard it's supposed to be funny. Maybe go for a pizza after."

"Sounds good to me."

Now, Maya was waiting in the lobby of the theatre, the first to arrive — her mom had dropped her off, and had told her to call her to be picked up if no one else could give her a lift home. She was cursing herself for not thinking of coming with Caitlin, because she hated sitting here all alone. What if David arrived next? She didn't know what he looked like, except a bit like Johnny Depp, which wasn't much help. And who should pay for the movie tickets? Was everyone paying for themselves, because it was supposed to be casual? Or would the guys want to be macho and pay? Or should Maya pay for Kirk, since she was the one who asked him out? With any luck, Caitlin would arrive first, and she could ask her opinion.

Just then the door opened, and Caitlin and a dark-haired guy came in together, laughing and holding hands.

"There she is!" called Caitlin. "Maya! We were waiting outside! Where's Kirk?"

"He's not here yet. Unless he's outside, too."

"I didn't see anyone else waiting. Maya, this is David."

"Hi, David," said Maya. She looked him over. Caitlin was right, he was quite good-looking, with thick, dark hair and big eyes. She reminded Maya not so much of Johnny Depp, but more like a languorous, taller version of Joey, with maybe a little bit of Claude thrown in, but she hadn't seen *Edward Scissorhands* yet. He wore his hair short in back, with thick bangs in front, and was dressed in Dockers and a soft cotton shirt, with Topsiders and no socks on his feet.

Caitlin had dashed back to see if she could see Kirk waiting, and now she returned, shaking her head. "I didn't see anyone who looked like he was waiting," she reported.

Maya glanced at her watch. "Well, it's a few minutes till the movie starts."

"Why don't we go in, and Maya and Kirk can join us?" said David, turning to Caitlin.

"No, we can't leave her by herself," objected Caitlin. "Besides, they'll never find us."

David leaned over and kissed Caitlin on the neck. "That's the idea," he muttered, obviously thinking that Maya hadn't heard him.

Caitlin giggled and twisted away. Maya tried to act like nothing unusual was going on. Where was Kirk?

The door opened again, but it was just another movie-going couple.

"Maybe I should call him," said Maya. "Maybe he got held up."

"Good idea," agreed Caitlin.

Maya fished in her purse for a quarter and buzzed over to the bank of phones on the far wall. Caitlin followed her. She flipped up the white pages, and turned to the name Buchanan. She didn't know what Kirk's father's name was, but there were only two columns of Buchanans, and she knew the address, or at least the street. But she skimmed over the columns two or three times, and there was no Buchanan on Morris St.

"That's funny," said Maya. "He doesn't seem to be in here."

"Maybe they moved recently," suggested Caitlin.

"No, because Kirk once said something about climbing in through the milkbox when he was a kid. He showed me the milkbox."

"Maybe their phone's unlisted," said Caitlin.

"I guess, but why?"

"Guys, the movie's about to start," said David, coming up, and putting his arm around Caitlin. "We should go in."

Maya looked pleadingly at Caitlin. She didn't want to be left out here all alone. What if he never showed? Her mom, she knew, was at a meeting at synagogue until later. She didn't want to sit in this brightly-lit lobby for the next two hours, to have everyone feel sorry for the little crippled girl who didn't have a date.

"We'll tell the ticket seller to watch for him and tell Kirk to join us," said Caitlin. "I'm sure he'll be here any minute."

"Shouldn't we wait just a few more minutes?" asked Maya. "Or, maybe you could lend me cab money, and I could just go home."

Now Caitlin gave Maya a pleading look. Oh yeah. She didn't want to be alone with David too much. Maya knew Caitlin would have done it for her. Probably. Should it ever arise ever in her entire life. Maya was utterly miserable. Stood up on her first date. And now, her friend needed her to do something for her.

"Come on, guys, we'll miss the beginning," urged David. "Or Maya, I could lend you cab fare, if you really don't want to stay."

Maya looked at each of them, and gave in. Yeah, she could be the third, fourth, fifth and sixth wheel on Caitlin and David's date. They went into the theatre.

Maya paid her own way.

The usher showed Maya where she could park herself, just behind the last row. Caitlin and David sat immediately in front of her. The trailers were over, and the movie was just beginning. A clown was walking along a street in New York. Maybe Kirk would still turn up.

Something about robbing a bank. While the audience laughed, Maya fought back the tears. In front of her, David kept snuggling up to Caitlin, and Caitlin kept squirming away. Along the row, another couple was making out. On the screen, a carload of bank robbers was lost in the grungiest part of town. By now, it was obvious Kirk wasn't coming. Stood up on her first date. She kept trying to convince herself there was an explanation, but she knew perfectly well what it was. He didn't want to be seen with her. It was all falling into place. How romantic he was when they were alone, but in public, he never held her hand, or kissed her goodbye. How he didn't want to stay for dinner, and get involved in her family. How she had never met his family or his friends. How no one at work had any idea they were together. Because they weren't. She had even co-operated on that one, by being coy when Sarah Anne had commented. He probably felt good about himself, being so enlightened as to be friends with a girl who used a wheelchair. Oh, yeah, it looked great that he always talked to her like a normal person at work. The making out sessions were either him taking pity on her, figuring she wouldn't get it anywhere else, or just an opportunity to get what he could from her — a few cheap thrills. But date her? Have a relationship with her? No way.

Maya was all the more deeply hurt because she had trusted him. He was so nice, so funny. He'd probably even have a plausible excuse, and continue being nice to her at work, but she knew the truth. The realization that Kirk was embarassed to be seen as her boyfriend felt like physical pain. Everyone in the theatre was laughing. On screen, Bill Murray seemed to be trying to buy something in a store, but she'd paid so little attention to the movie, she had no idea what was going on. She hurt so much. She let herself cry. If anyone said anything, she could just say she'd laughed so hard, she'd cried. How come no one ever cried so hard they laughed?

By the time the movie was over, Maya had pulled herself sort of together, and gathered what she could find of her pride. She didn't care what Caitlin said, she had to go home.

"So what do you say, guys?" Caitlin was saying as they made their way through the lobby. "Pizza? I don't have to be home for another hour."

"Um, Caitlin, I think I'd just as soon go home, if you don't mind," said Maya. "I'm pretty tired. It's nice of you to ask me, though."

Caitlin gave her the pleading look again, but Maya just couldn't come through for her friend any more.

"But Maya, I want you and David to get to know each other," said Caitlin.

"She said she's tired," said David. "I can give you a drive home, if you like, Maya," he offered.

"That would be nice," said Maya. "Thank you, David."

Maya was quiet on the ride home, and when she got in, she went straight to bed. Bubbie had stopped her and asked about the date, and Maya had lied and said it went fine. Bubbie gave her a funny look, but didn't question her further. Tucked in bed, with the covers pulled up over her head, Maya buried her face in her pillow and sobbed and sobbed and sobbed.

In the morning, her eyes stinging and puffy, Maya wheeled reluctantly to work. She didn't want a scene with Kirk at work, so she tried to be around other people as much as she could all day. At lunch, she ate quickly, and took off to the drugstore before Kirk came out. She looked at lipsticks for fifteen minutes. Maybe she should start wearing more makeup. Maya selected a rich red lipstick, which she put on before returning to work just as her lunch break ended. Fortunately, the afternoon was busy, so the extent of her conversation with everyone was "Ketchup, lettuce, mayo, mustard, onions, pickles, relish, tomatoes," and "Order in!"

When her shift ended, Maya hung up her uniform and left the store as quickly as she could. She had managed never to meet Kirk's eye all day, though she sensed he wanted to talk to her. Fine. Let him see how it felt. But as she buzzed along the street homeward, she heard running footsteps behind her, and Kirk's voice calling her name. She kept going. Let him catch up.

He ran past and stopped in front of her. Maya veered her chair to go around him, but he cut her off.

"Wait," he ordered, catching his breath. "Wait, I'm sorry. Let me explain."

Maya folded her arms across her chest and looked at him.

Seeing he had her grudging attention, Kirk went on. "Look, I'm sorry about last night," he said. "I — my dad — is kind of sick. He gets dizzy. He got dizzy last night, just when I was about to come to the theatre, I couldn't leave. I knew you'd have already left, and I didn't know how to call you at the theatre. So — I hoped you wouldn't be too mad at me. I'm sorry."

"You could have called my house. At least then I would have known last night." Maya was starting to melt. Kirk's excuse sounded far-fetched, but it could be true.

"I told you, I couldn't leave my dad."

"I tried to call you. You're not in the phone book."

"No, um, our number's unlisted. Because of my dad's shifts, you know, he doesn't like to get wakened up in the day by sales calls. They can't call you if you're un-listed."

That was it. Maya knew Kirk was lying. There was something weird, something he wasn't telling her. His dad was dizzy, he was sleeping, he worked in a factory, their number was unlisted. He had to stay home with his father, where was his mother? He couldn't call her house because he couldn't leave his dad. Yet he was going to be leav-ing for out west in the fall. It just didn't add up.

"Don't lie to me Kirk," she spat out. "I don't know which part is the lie, but I know you're lying. The truth is, you're just ashamed to be seen with me. You're all amorous and everything when we're alone, but as soon as we're in public, it's brother and sister time. I've never met your family, I've never met any of your friends, *if* you have any. You never tell me anything about yourself, not really, not information, not facts. You've never even told me you like me. I used to think it was because you were shy. But now I think you're just using me."

"No, Maya, it's not like that at all. Believe me. Look, please don't be like this," Kirk pleaded. "I do like you."

"Yeah. As a friend. So you can look good befriending the little crippled girl. You don't like me. You pity me. Well, I don't need your pity. Get out of my way, I'm going home."

Maya stared at him, at those eyes she used to think were so tender. Now, he just looked helpless. After a moment, he looked away, then stepped aside. Maya pushed the lever on the arm of her wheelchair and shot forward, daring her tears to fall.

# Chapter 10

After her fight with Kirk, work was more of a routine than a pleasure. Sure, it was all money toward the van conversion and driving lessons, and the rest of the gang were still fun to be around. But now, without Kirk's eye to catch, a secret smile to exchange, work was just ketchup, lettuce, mayonnaise, mustard, onions, pickles, relish, tomatoes, order in, order up sixty-four, the striped tunic, two-sixty-three please and thirty-seven cents change thank you sir.

Scotty's off-colour jokes and suggestive remarks hadn't lessened since she had started wearing the tank top under her uniform. Maya made a career out of avoiding being alone with him and his too-neat hair and his too-dapper navy suit.

Kirk announced that he had rejigged the lunch schedule to give everyone a change, so now Maya's overlapped with Grace's.

The other girls must have been disappointed that he had scheduled his own break to coincide with halves of Tommy's and Kei-Kei's lunches. The one oddly nice thing about this was that it was obvious to Maya that he had made the change to avoid spending time with her — which meant that maybe he *had* put them together on purpose in the first place. Kirk didn't act very differently around her — the other staff would have had no more idea that they had broken up (as if they'd ever been together) than that they had been more than friends in the first place (if in fact they had been). The only odd thing was that Maya felt like he was watching her a lot, like he always wanted to know where she was. During the first half of her lunch break, when she was alone, he almost always went past the staff lounge, or if she was out at the picnic table, he came out with a bag of garbage for the dumpster. He never said anything about it, always acted casual, but it made her feel strange.

The summer was half over, and Caitlin and Maya's big summer plans seemed to be going nowhere, mostly. Caitlin was still seeing David, and so far had mostly managed to keep things from going any further than second base, mainly by always refusing the wine that David persisted in bringing on their dates. They were fighting a lot about sex, and Caitlin had to admit to Maya that she was sort of fighting about it inside, which probably meant she was giving David mixed signals. She really wanted to find out what it was like, but wasn't sure she wanted to lose the big V to David. She loved him, she loved him not. Caitlin was sympathetic to Maya about the break-up, if you could call it that, with Kirk, breezily assuring Maya that men were like buses. If you miss one, another one will be along in a moment. Didn't Caitlin remember that buses were like men — inaccessible if you used a wheelchair?

The driving thing hadn't come to much, either. Caitlin was continuing her lessons so she could get in more practice, but she was taking them sporadically, as she could afford to pay for them. Maya had managed to save a fair bit toward the van conversion, but there was the cost of the lessons too, and she didn't have enough to start them yet.

Even Maya's poems were hackneyed garbage, riddled with clichés.

The only things that brought Maya much pleasure these days were reading, and watching old movies on video. Maya and Bubbie often rented an old musher or a comedy, and, armed with popcorn, sat on

Bubbie's bed and watched them. Bubbie would tell Maya all about the first time she'd seen *Casablanca* and who she'd gone with, and how Ingrid Bergman had had a baby and she wasn't married, and hardly worked in Hollywood again, and how Lauren Bacall met Humphrey Bogart on the set of *To Have and Have Not* when she was just a teenager, and later they got married.

"You're not seeing that boy Kirk any more?" Bubbie asked her.

Maya shook her head. She didn't think she wanted to talk to Bubbie about it. She knew Bubbie had been young once, but things were different for Maya, and she didn't think Bubbie would understand.

"Does it make you sad?"

Maya shook her head again.

"There was a boy in school I liked, but he didn't even know I existed — Sam Neiman. Finally I got the chance to meet him. My friends nearly forced him to ask me to the dance. We didn't have a very good time. But I met his best friend there — Ben Levy — your Zaide. Ben played in a band. We fell in love and got married. We were poor, but happy. You know what happened to Sam?"

Maya had heard the story a million times before, but she shook her head again.

"He got rich. Made his fortune in toilet

plungers. Sure, people need them, but how can you love a man like that? He wears a little gold plunger on his lapel. Three different wives he's had — so far. So, *shayna maidl*, you never know."

Maya smiled at her grandmother. On the screen, Humphrey Bogart was sitting alone in Rick's Café Americain, telling Sam to play it.

And then it would be back to Slurps the next day and avoiding Kirk's watchful eye, and trying to only go to the storeroom when Scotty was somewhere else.

One day at the beginning of August, Maya noticed that the straw dispensers were empty at the front, and she pointed it out to Sarah Anne.

"Would you mind getting the straws?" she asked. "They're on a shelf too high for me. I'll put them in the dispensers."

"Sure," agreed Sarah Anne, and headed for the storeroom.

Maya noticed Scotty, who had been adjusting some signs in the window, went along the hall, too.

Sarah Anne was gone a surprisingly long time, for someone who was just getting straws. When she did return, she looked upset, and thrust the straws at Maya without a word. Grabbing a damp cloth from behind the counter, she headed to the front of the restaurant and began scrubbing the tables like she was trying to wear holes in them. Scotty had not returned.

"Sarah Anne?" Maya asked her.

The beads on Sarah Anne's cornrowed hair clacked together as she swung her head around sharply. "What?" she snapped.

"Is — something wrong?"

"No," said Sarah Anne, "why should anything be wrong? The tables needed cleaning." Sarah Anne smiled, but her smile was brittle.

Scotty emerged from the back of the restaurant, smoothing back his hair with his hand. "Good to see you girls keeping the place nice," he commended them.

Sarah abruptly returned to her scrubbing, and Maya began to fill the dispensers. Kirk, from the kitchen, was watching Scotty as he returned to his office. Maya wondered what was going on. Had Scotty been spying on Sarah Anne, too? But she was only getting straws, what was there to see? It didn't make sense to Maya, but something was definitely weird.

Only a few days later, Maya found out what. This time, it was the napkin dispensers that needed filling. The napkins were on a low shelf in the storeroom, so Maya went to get them herself, first checking that Scotty wasn't around anywhere.

"I'm getting napkins," she said to Sarah Anne as she wheeled down the hall. "Be right back." She felt Kirk's eyes on her as she buzzed past the kitchen.

The napkins came in paper packages that were shipped inside of larger cardboard boxes. Maya discovered that she would have to open a fresh box to get a package of the napkins. The box was lying on its side, sealed with brown paper packing tape. Maya pulled at it, but she couldn't tear it, so she glanced around for some sort of knife or sharp edge she could use.

"Want some help?" asked Scotty, from the doorway. Maya shuddered. She'd managed to do what she had avoided for weeks — find herself alone with Scotty. Still, he was only offering help with the box. What was the harm in that? She continued to pull at the tape.

Scotty crossed the room behind her and leaned over the side of her wheelchair. Steadying the box with his left hand, he took a set of keys from his pocket with the right, and used one to slit the packing tape. As he leaned further over, to continue tearing the tape across the top of the box, Maya thought he had chosen a rather awkward way to work on the box, with her in the way. Until she realized that something hard was pushing into her shoulder. She leaned away, but he followed. Scotty was deliberately pushing his crotch into her shoulder! Maya's mouth went dry, and she moved her arm to reach for the lever on her chair, to back away.

"Hey, don't do that," said Scotty, in a coaxing tone of voice. "An attractive young lady like you, it's time to learn about the ways of the world. I could be a great teacher." He took Maya's hand, pulling it toward him, but she twisted it loose, and backed up her chair.

"Don't!" she whispered, then swallowed to get her voice back. "Give me the napkins."

Scotty held out a package of napkins from the opened box. As she reached out to take them, he pulled them back. "Come and get them," he taunted her, stepping further back into the storeroom. But Maya grabbed another package from the box, and fled.

In the hallway, she tried to compose herself, to look normal around the others. She didn't want to let on, not until she'd sorted things out for herself. Methodically, she stuffed the napkin dispensers. She thought Kirk was looking at her, but when she looked up, he was carefully scraping the grill. Maya wished she and Kirk were

113

still friends. She would have given anything to have had someone to talk to about all of this.

Scotty didn't reappear for half an hour, and by then it was getting busy in the restaurant. Somehow, Maya managed to finish her shift, go home, and get through dinner and her chores by simply blocking out the whole incident.

But alone in her room, the thoughts, the questions, the emotions began to swirl around inside her head.

First, she thought about what had actually happened. Had she led Scotty on? Was it her red lipstick? But he'd spied on her — she was pretty sure — before she had the lipstick. And she'd been wearing it for a while now. Still, it was the first time they'd been alone since she'd gotten the lipstick. But the lipstick was ridiculous. If men were that crazed by red lipstick, no one would ever wear it in public. Had she laughed at any of his gross jokes? She didn't think so. Had she been friendly to him, or seemed to be? Did it have to do with the raise? Should she have turned it down? Did anything really happen? Did he maybe just lean on her by accident? Could it have been his fly, or something in his pocket that was hard? Don't be ridiculous, Maya, you know perfectly well you didn't lead him on, and he knew perfectly well what he was doing, and so do you, she told herself. His comment afterward made that clear.

But what to do? Obviously she should quit her job. How could she continue to work there, with Scotty around all the time? How could she face him? How could she do her work? But on the other hand, where was she going to get another summer job now? And she was *so close* to having enough money to start the driving lessons. It didn't seem fair, why should she be the one to quit, when he was the one who started it? She was pretty sure of two things, now, anyway. Scotty *had* been watching her get changed before — even if she'd had any doubt. And it probably happened to Sarah Anne, too, that day with the straws. And Sarah Anne had stuck it out. So could she. This was the first time that her wheelchair had made her feel helpless, though. It was hard to get away, it was hard to manœuvre. But little though she wanted to, she could stick out the summer, just to get her driving lessons. What a truly rotten summer this had turned out to be.

If only there were someone she could talk to about it all. Sarah Anne was obviously not going to talk, and Kirk was out of the picture. She couldn't talk to her parents or Bubbie about something like this — it would only upset them, and they'd make her quit, and then she'd never learn to drive. And Caitlin was ... Caitlin.

Maya did get together with Caitlin the following evening, after an uncomfortable day at work. Fortunately, Scotty didn't say anything to her, but she was aware of him being around. She had such a feeling of being spied on that, even if she knew he was back in his office, she felt like he could see her, was watching her. And Kirk was still watching her too. Was she turning paranoid in her old age?

Maya escaped at the end of the day, and when Caitlin breezed by later on, Maya was grateful. She could always count on Caitlin's daily melodramas to bring her out of herself and put things into perspective.

When the two girls were alone, Maya said the magic spell that always got Caitlin going. "How's David?"

As usual, it worked.

"David! Don't talk to me about David. He's getting really pushy, Maya. A couple of nights ago, he had wine again, as usual, and as usual, instead of going to the movies, we went straight to the bluffs. He got really mad that I wouldn't drink any of the wine, so I had a little, and we got to third base again. Anyway, then he really started getting pushy last night. He kept

116

saying all that stuff about if I loved him I would, and he'd turn blue or something, and I was a tease after he bought all that wine and paid for the gas — the gas! — in his father's car — that I owed him! As if I'm a prostitute or something! Anyway, we had a big fight, and then he said he was sorry, and we made up, and it started getting really hot again, but fortunately, it was getting late, so I had to go home."

"The creep!" agreed Maya. "As if he bought you with gasoline!"

"But I don't know, Maya," Caitlin went on in a different voice. "When he's sweet, he's so sweet, and we used to have a lot of fun, before we started fighting about sex all the time. I'm scared he might dump me, and he *is* cute, and I *would* like to know what — you know — all the fuss is about."

"But do you love him?" asked Maya.

"I don't know," conceded Caitlin. "Sometimes I think I do. But sometimes I don't even like him. I mean, sometimes he just acts like he owns me. We go out in that boat of a car of his dad's and it's all plushy inside, well, you saw it, and we always go where *he* wants to go, and it sometimes feels like — I feel trapped."

"Caitlin, he has no right to expect anything you don't want to give him," said Maya firmly. "Any more than Scotty does."

117

Oops. Maya had been struck by the parallels in the two situations, but she hadn't meant to say anything.

"Scotty?" said Caitlin. "Isn't he your boss? What does he have to do with it?"

"Nothing," said Maya quickly.

"What do you mean, nothing?" asked Caitlin sharply. "I know you, Maya, you meant something."

Maya was quiet for a moment, but then decided, why not tell Caitlin? Maybe she'd have some good advice. But she knew what the good advice was going to be — quit the job, and Maya couldn't afford to. But she did need to talk to someone, to help her get her thoughts straight.

"I wasn't going to say anything," Maya began quietly, "but the other day, I was in the storeroom, getting napkins for the dispensers ... " And Maya told Caitlin everything, including the spying, and the rude jokes, and the raise, and the part about the long-sleeved top and the air conditioning, and her suspicions that the same thing was happening to Sarah Anne, and maybe other girls too.

Caitlin listened to the whole story, occasionally gasping or squeaking in dismay or outrage.

"So, I've been thinking I should quit, but I don't want to," Maya finished up.

"Quit?!" cried Caitlin. "Are you nuts? You

118

have to report this guy. You can't let him
get away with it! He can't do this to you!"

"Report him?" echoed Maya. She had
never even thought of it. Maya had
thought it was simply a question of quitting or staying. But report him? It was an
idea.

# Chapter 11

"But how do I do it?" asked Maya. "I mean, even if I decide to report him, who do I report him to?"

"I don't know," replied Caitlin. "Head Office?"

"Yeah," said Maya thoughtfully. Then, "Caitlin, I don't know if I can do it."

"You can't not," urged Caitlin.

"But — what if they don't believe me? I mean, it's my word against his, right? He's the manager, I'm just a counter-girl."

"Yeah, but why would you make it up?"

"Who knows? But why would — I mean, *I* don't think he's good-looking, but some people would — why would a good-looking guy hit on a girl in a wheelchair?"

"Maya, you have to stop putting yourself down. You always say that, but there's nothing wrong with you — you're pretty, you're nice, you're smart."

"That's very sweet, Caitlin, but you know

what I mean," said Maya. "Most people would think I'd be grateful for the attention. Like David seems to act about you and gasoline."

In spite of the seriousness of the situation, both girls broke out laughing.

"I tell you what," giggled Maya. "Offer to pay him gas money to stay at first base."

"And you give Scotty a raise if he promises not to try anything with you." Caitlin joined in.

This set them off on more gales of laughter. When they stopped laughing, Maya felt better than she had felt in weeks. "I'll make a deal with you," she said. "I'll report Scotty if you dump David."

Caitlin thought about it for a moment. "You're right," she finally said. "He's not worth it. It's not even fun any more, it's nothing but fooling around and fighting."

Next day was Maya's day off again, so it was the perfect opportunity to call Slurps Head Office. If only Caitlin hadn't been working that day. It was so much easier to believe she was doing the right thing with Caitlin there. It was so hard to get up the nerve. And she had to do it before noon, because that was when Bubbie and Mom and Janna and Joel would be back for lunch from swimming lessons, grocery shopping, and Bubbie's Knit and Chat at the community centre.

It had seemed so easy when Caitlin said it, but who should she actually call? What would she say? Caitlin was always getting in trouble for trying to do the right thing — maybe this was just another one of her crazy ideas.

Maya stalled, washing her hair, making her bed (her mother would flip!), staring at the phone, sorting the mail when it arrived. Every time she reached out for the phone, she got a sharp sinking feeling in her stomach, like an elevator going down too fast, and she pulled her hand away. The clock on the microwave clicked over to 11:39. She had twenty-one minutes to get the call over with, or when would she ever do it? Maya muttered a quick prayer to herself, a snippet remembered from Hebrew school, picked up the phone and dialled the number. Even now she could still back out, but she held on to the phone, listened to it ring. She knew where it was ringing, it was where she had waited for her interview six weeks ago. Gosh, was it only six weeks? So much had happened since then.

"Slurps, how can I help you?" came the voice.

"Um, yes, may I have the personnel department, please?" Maya figured that was the place to start.

"One moment."

She could still hang up, she could, no one would ever know it was her calling. She gripped the phone receiver tightly in her hand. She would go through with this, she had to.

"Personnel, Nancy speaking."

Nancy! She remembered Nancy. She was the one who had spoken to her that very first time. Maya decided not to give her name, not right away.

"Um, hello, uh, I'm an employee in one of your restaurants, and I was wondering what would happen if, like, one of the managers was coming on to an employee?" Come on, Maya, they weren't going to fall for the hypothetical thing.

"We would want to know about it right away," said Nancy. "Can you give me any more details?"

Maya relaxed. She knew Nancy was one of the good guys. It was going to be okay.

Nancy took down everything over the phone, and then made an appointment to see Maya after work the following day, in The Donut Shoppe, down the road from Slurps. She promised Maya that Scotty would not be told who had reported him, though Maya figured he could make an educated guess, unless he was hitting on every female employee in the place —

123

which maybe he was. Maya managed to have the table set for lunch before the others got back. She decided not to say anything to her family right away. If only she could talk to Caitlin, but that wouldn't be until tomorrow night, because tonight, she was going to be breaking up with David. So she said.

When Maya arrived at work the following morning, the place was buzzing. Obviously, something was up. A stylish young woman in an attractive sand-coloured suit and an ice-blue silk shirt called all the staff into the kitchen.

"Your manager, Mr. MacFarland, has been transferred to head office." she announced. "You will be getting a new manager soon, but in the meantime, I will be filling in. My name's Amanda Simon. Kirk Buchanan will remain shift manager, everything continues just as before. If you have any problems or questions at all, my door is always open."

Grace raised her hand tentatively. "Is Scotty okay?" she asked.

"Yes, he's fine," said Amanda, smiling. "It's just a personnel thing, a rearrangement of staffing."

Maya was astonished. Was he gone because of her? She had no idea things would happen so fast. And if he was gone, why did she have to meet with Nancy today? Had he been fired? Or was he promoted?

The day flew by. Maya and Sarah Anne joked with the customers. Sarah Anne hummed to herself as she polished napkin dispensers. In the kitchen, people laughed, and Grace and Tommy did a hilarious rendition of "Under the Boardwalk" during the after-lunch lull, Grace singing the bass line, while Tommy sang a falsetto soprano. For Maya, it was as though she had sprouted wings. The oppressive feeling of being watched all the time was gone, and she noticed that even though Kirk still glanced at her occasionally, he wasn't dogging her every move. He didn't even check on her at lunch time, like he usually did. She actually sort of wished he had. Even though she knew he was a creep, she kind of missed him a little.

After work, she changed quickly, and headed for The Donut Shoppe, where Nancy was already waiting.

"Hello, Maya," Nancy greeted her. "Would you like something to drink, or a donut?"

"Just a Coke would be nice, please," said Maya.

After the Coke arrived, Nancy folded her hands on top of the table.

"Well, Maya, as you can see, your phone call has brought quick results."

Maya nodded.

"But I'm afraid we do have to ask you some more questions. We can't punish a man just on your say-so, we have to be sure that what you say happened really did."

Maya nodded again, and swallowed. So it wasn't over. They didn't believe her.

"Now, the easiest thing would be if someone else came forward and said the same thing happened to them. Do you know of anyone else it happened to? Did any of the other girls — or boys — say anything?"

"I think something happened with Sarah Anne," said Maya.

"Did she tell you that?"

"No, but one day, she was in the storeroom, and Scotty followed her and she came back upset. She wouldn't say anything, though, when I asked if she was okay."

"Did you see Scotty go into the storeroom? Could he have gone somewhere else?"

"He could have, it was just that she was upset, and there wasn't any reason I could see other than that. Maybe if she knew I said something, she would too."

"Any others?"

Maya shook her head.

"Okay," said Nancy.

"What about the spying?" asked Maya.

"Well, that's even trickier," said Nancy. "It sounded on the phone like you weren't sure he was really doing that."

"Well, I wasn't *sure*. But when he got upset with me for wearing the long sleeves, it seemed like ... " Maya trailed off. It wasn't exactly proof, like in a court of law. She'd seen *Street Legal*. Even though she knew he'd done it, she knew there was no real evidence, just her word against his. And she was back where she started, like she'd said to Caitlin — who was going to believe her?

Nancy must have noticed her expression, because she looked sympathetically at Maya. "Look, Maya," she reassured her. "It took courage to come forward with this, and we appreciate it. Don't worry. We'll be asking Scotty lots of questions, too. We just want to make sure this is resolved in the fairest way possible. I'll be in touch." They didn't believe her.

Maya looked out the window at the passing pedestrians. Kirk was one of them, on his way to get his dad's car from the parking lot, Maya figured. He didn't seem to see her, and walked on. They didn't believe her.

Caitlin and Maya agreed to meet in the

playground that evening to talk about everything that had been happening. While they could usually get privacy at one of their houses, they couldn't guarantee it, and tonight they definitely needed privacy.

"How did it go with David?" Maya asked, when they were settled, Caitlin with her feet up on a park bench. Not far away, little kids were splashing in the wading pool as the shadows lengthened on a sticky summer evening.

"Well," said Caitlin, getting comfortable to tell her story. "I decided to do a kind of a test. If he would listen, and treat me properly, I'd give him another chance. So, when he came, he said, as usual, 'Let's skip the movie, and go down to the bluffs.' And I said, no, I really wanted to see the movie — it was *Kindergarten Cop* — Maya, you'd love the little kids, they're all exactly like Joel."

"Yeah, yeah," said Maya, smiling. Caitlin could never get straight to the point. "Get on with it."

"Okay, so then I bought us popcorn, and then after, I said we should go for a Coke, but he wanted to go to the bluffs. So I said, okay, we can go to the bluffs, but only kissing, no wine, no second base, no third base. So we got there, and we're parked, and he has the radio on, and we start making out and stuff, and he pulls out the wine, and I reminded him, no wine, so he made a face and put it away. Then, he goes straight for my leg, and he's trying to get his hand up my skirt, and I'm pushing him away. I stopped kissing him, and I said, 'Look, David, I like you and everything, but, really, I don't want to go so far.' Anyway, he got really mad, and he called me a word I can't even say, which was the opposite of what he meant and started with an 's', and said how he paid for the movie and I said I paid for the popcorn, and he said he paid for the gas, and I told him he didn't buy me, and if he didn't like it, he could take me home. He peeled out of there, he was really mad. To tell you the truth, I was a little scared, but he took me home, and I got out, and said, 'Don't call me,' and he said, 'In your dreams.' And that's that. He didn't 'What ho' me at work today. It's a lucky thing Yorktown Village is so spread out. I felt sort of bad making him take me to the movie, knowing I was probably going to dump him, but if he wants to make the whole thing a monetary transaction, I figure *he* owes *me*. So what do you think?"

Maya was grinning. "Yahoo!" she cried. "Chalk one up for the good guys!"

"Okay," said Caitlin. "Your turn. Did you call?"

"I called, Caitlin," said Maya. "And he's gone."

"Gone!? Just like that? That's wonderful!" exclaimed Caitlin.

"Well, sort of," replied Maya. "They've moved him to Head Office. When you think about it, it's sort of like he got a promotion. Today, I had to talk to Nancy, from Personnel, after work. I'm not sure they believe me."

"They *have* to believe you! It's true!" said Caitlin, outraged.

Trust good old Caitlin. When it came right down to it, she'd always go to the wall for what she thought was right, for her friends. Maya smiled a wry smile.

"Well, they keep asking if there were any witnesses or anyone else it happened to. I told them Sarah Anne, but unless *she* says it, it's no good."

"So talk to Sarah Anne. Tell her she has to come forward too."

"I can try it, I guess," said Maya. But she was pretty sure she knew what Sarah Anne's answer would be.

# Chapter 12

Maya tackled Sarah Anne before the lunch-time rush the next day. The girls were stocking up the sugar, salt and pepper packets.

"Sarah Anne," Maya spoke quietly. "Do you know why Scotty's gone?"

"I don't know, and I don't care," said Sarah Anne, blithely. "I'm just glad he is, and I hope he doesn't come back."

"Me too," answered Maya. "But I know why he's gone."

"I don't listen to gossip," replied Sarah Anne.

"This isn't gossip," insisted Maya. "Sarah Anne, he left because I turned him in. I told on him for hitting on me in the store-room. He hit on you too, didn't he?"

"No, he did not."

"Sarah Anne, I know he did, the day I asked you to get the straws." Maya's voice was urgent. "Listen, you have to tell them, too. I don't think they believe me. You have to back me up."

"He did not hit on me," said Sarah Anne again. "And even if he did, I'm keeping my mouth shut."

"Sarah Anne, you've got to speak up. You can't let him get away with it." Maya's tone was getting desperate.

"You don't know my dad," said Sarah Anne, fixing Maya with a stare. "If he ever found out, he'd be furious with me."

"Furious with *you*? You didn't do anything!"

"Maya, I must have done something to lead him on. I don't know what it was, but I'm just glad he's gone."

"You didn't lead him on. I didn't lead him on. He's a creep. But if they don't believe me, he might come back."

"If he does, then I'll just have to quit, I guess," said Sarah Anne. "Because he's going to know somebody here turned him in."

"But Sarah Anne, we can fight it," argued Maya. "You don't have to quit."

"No." Sarah Anne picked up the box of sugar packages and moved to the next condiment station. Maya didn't bother to follow her.

Sarah Anne was quiet for the rest of the morning, but the atmosphere in the kitchen remained buoyant. Grace was carrying on and singing so much, Maya thought she was in danger of getting fired. Maybe Grace was just relieved. Maybe Scotty had hit on her, too. Maya would ask her at lunch time. She just had to get someone to back up her story.

When the lunch-time crowd died down, Maya took her break. She wheeled out, as usual, to the picnic table behind the restaurant. The sun was warm, and there was a light breeze rustling the leaves above. Maya didn't have any sunscreen on, but she didn't think a few minutes would do her any real harm, and she turned her already tanned face into the sun and closed her eyes.

Maya felt herself almost drifting off, when a voice very close to her ear said quietly, "You little tart." Her eyes snapped open, and she found herself looking at Scotty's perfect white teeth.

Maya wheeled backward a few inches.

"What are you doing here?" she gasped. She was quickly trying to assess the situation. Could she get away, if she had to? The door back into the restaurant opened outward, tricky for her to negotiate quickly in her chair, even though it was propped open a few inches. If she screamed, she doubted anyone would notice much — kids played back here all the time. Why weren't they here now? Grace wasn't due on lunch for at least ten minutes. There was no one else in the laneway behind the stores. Could she get into any of the other stores from here? Maya didn't know. Or could she get out onto the sidestreet? Maybe. That seemed like the best bet. But, so far, Scotty didn't seem to be trying anything.

He was wearing his navy suit, his tie slightly loosened, perhaps because of the warm day. He looked as smooth and well-turned out as ever, shoes polished, hair combed back. Maya didn't know why she was surprised by this — he was working at Head Office, after all. Somehow, she had been picturing him as dishevelled, maybe unshaven, a man broken by Nancy's questioning. But here he was, the same old Scotty, smiling, even.

"You little tart," he said again. "Think you're clever, don't you? Well, it's your word against mine, my dear, even if anything did happen. And you know perfectly well it didn't. What can you prove? Nothing. No witnesses. Because nothing happened."

"You call that nothing?" asked Maya. She knew it was a pretty lame comment, but she was trying to buy time. Her best hope was that he would leave, or that Grace would come out before anything awful happened.

"Come on, you know you have a great fantasy life. You have to, you can't get around like the other girls can, you've developed your imagination. It's understandable."

Maya was turning white hot with anger. How dare he suggest she imagined his creepy stuff! If she were going to imagine something, she would make sure it would be a lot better than that!

"You're the one with the fantasy life," she spat back at him. "You think you're God's gift to women." Maya knew she might make him angry, and that was stupid, but she couldn't help herself.

Scotty's tone changed, his smile vanished, for perhaps the first time ever in Maya's experience. "Listen, you little —" Scotty used a word that, although Maya knew existed, she'd never actually heard anyone call another person before. "You should count your lucky stars *anyone* wants you. You think that wheelchair makes you sexy? You should have taken it from me — you're not going to get it from anyone else. No one else is going to be interested in you."

"That's what you believe, Scotty?" said a quiet voice behind Maya. Maya swung around to see Kirk standing in the doorway. He tossed the bag of garbage he was holding into the dumpster. "Well, you're

135

wrong. *I'm* interested in her. In fact, we're going together, for your information." Maya looked at Kirk in surprise. Going together? They had barely spoken to each other in two weeks. Obviously, he was saying it to defend her, but it was funny that when they *were* together, he would never acknowledge it, but now that they weren't, he said they were. Kirk, now standing behind her, put his hands on Maya's shoulders. They felt warm, and electric, like back before things went wrong. "She's nice, and she's smart, and she's pretty, and if you can't see it, you're stupid."

Maya couldn't help wishing that she could believe Kirk meant it, and couldn't believe she was thinking about Kirk instead of Scotty, who was standing, at a loss for words, in front of them.

"I know what you've been doing to the girls who work here," Kirk went on. "And I'm glad you're gone. I hope they fire you."

"You knew?" gasped Maya. He knew and he didn't say anything, didn't warn her?

"Maya, why don't you finish your lunch break inside," Kirk dismissed her, stepping around her wheelchair toward Scotty.

"I'll fight my own battles, thank you very much," Maya snapped at him, and turned back to Scotty, who was looking at them both with a surprised expression on his

136

face. "There. Now there's a witness. You're sunk. Get out of here before I call the police. You're not supposed to be here."

Suddenly Scotty retreated, holding up his hands, palms facing outward, backing off.

Maya turned towards Kirk. "You should have gone inside," he was saying. "He might have done something to you."

"Don't order me around," she snapped back. "He already did, remember?"

"I was just looking out for you," Kirk defended himself. "You're lucky I came out."

"Looking out for me? You might have thought of warning me before anything even happened. Everyone seems to think I'm lucky I know them today. Must be my lucky day," she finished, sarcastically.

"I tried to watch out — I never really thought he'd do anything to *you*," was Kirk's reply.

"Why? Because of my wheelchair?"

"Well … "

"He didn't do it because he was attracted to me, you know," said Maya in a dark voice. "He did it because he thought he could get away with it. I can see how attractive *you* find me — nice of you to lie to Scotty and get to be the knight in shining armour." Maya almost choked on the last words. She felt so hurt, so patronized, so angry, she thought she might cry. Grabbing her lunch bag off the picnic table, she headed toward the door of the restaurant. She hated doors that opened towards her.

"Maya, you've got it all wrong," came Kirk's voice behind her, soft and dusty and sad.

Maya ignored him. She stopped her chair, and grasped the handle, flinging the door wide to give her enough time to start through. But, in her anger, she swung too hard, and the door came banging back instantly. Taking a slow breath to calm herself down, Maya reached for the handle again.

"Maya, I heard you talking to Sarah Anne." Kirk's voice was flat and resigned. "I know you need someone to back you up. What he said to you today was practically a confession. I'll be your witness."

Oh, great. Knight in shining armour time again. But she really did need him. "Thank you," she said, without looking at him. She reached again for the door handle, but Kirk was suddenly standing in front of the door, blocking her way. He looked angry.

"Look, what do you want from me?" he snapped. "I'm offering to help. I told you I tried to watch out."

"I *said* thank you," said Maya, equally crossly. "What do you want, a medal? Nice of you to take pity on me."

"Pity. There you go with that word again. Don't you get it? I meant what I said, you know. I do think you're smart and pretty and nice. And brave. But you're too busy feeling sorry for yourself to think that anyone else could have a good opinion of you."

Maya was stung. The one thing she prided herself on was not feeling sorry for herself. How dare Kirk accuse her of self-pity? She was just realistic. Anyway, it didn't alter the facts.

"Well, if you think I'm so wonderful, how come you stood me up that time? How come you never wanted to be seen in public with me as a couple?"

"I told you — my dad was sick. But your mind was too made up to listen to me. You were too busy feeling sorry for yourself as usual. You want to be seen in public? Fine. Let's go to the movies tonight." Kirk spat the words at her, like a challenge. Maya took it up.

"Tonight? Fine," she snapped back. "Pick me up at seven."

"Fine." Kirk held the door for Maya as she returned to finish her shift. They didn't speak for the rest of the afternoon.

# Chapter 13

It was the oddest sensation, getting in the car with Kirk when he came to pick her up. She was still kind of mad at him, but she was also looking forward to spending the evening with him. She really had missed him, more than she had realized.

As they pulled away from her house, he turned and smiled at her. "I missed you, you know," he confessed. And the last of Maya's anger vanished like water on a hot frying pan.

They went to see *Kindergarten Cop*, and Caitlin was right, the kids were like Joel. Maya was grinning as they went out through the lobby, but Kirk seemed preoccupied, distant somehow.

"Want to go for pizza?" invited Maya. "My treat."

"Yeah, sure," said Kirk, but without much enthusiasm.

There was a pizza place just two doors

down from the theatre, and they headed towards it.

"What do you like?" Maya asked Kirk.

"Huh?" asked Kirk.

"On your pizza."

"Oh. Whatever you like. No pineapple, unless it's your favourite."

"I've often wondered who thought of putting pineapple on pizza in the first place," said Maya. "It's kind of like putting garlic on ice cream, to me."

Kirk smiled, but it didn't seem like he was really listening.

"You don't want to go for pizza, do you?" Maya asked him.

"Sure, pizza's fine," said Kirk. Then, "No, not really. I want to talk. Want to drive down to the bluffs? I mean — not to — just to talk?"

Kirk and Maya were both aware of the bluffs' reputation as a make-out place. But it was dark and private and pretty, and it was the perfect place to talk, or whatever.

They piled into Lady Godiva, now up and running, though looking like a badly-designed patchwork quilt. The trunk, of course, wouldn't close with Maya's wheelchair in it, and she wondered what anyone who saw them at the bluffs would think — because they'd have to know it was her. On the trip there, they didn't talk much. Maya looked at Kirk out of the side of her eye. He looked even more gorgeous than ever, the planes of his face illuminated occasionally as they passed under streetlamps. Tonight he had on his usual black jeans, and a black shirt with rust-coloured designs, made out of some soft fabric, maybe rayon, the long sleeves rolled partway up his arms. She glanced at his black cowboy boot as his foot moved from brake to accelerator. Soon, soon, she'd be driving too. Maya wondered if, now that the car was running, Kirk was still planning to leave. He must have sensed her looking at him, because he turned and smiled at her.

They arrived at the bluffs and parked, pointing out toward the lake, and Maya could see the lights sparkling on the water from a few late yachters. Kirk turned toward Maya, and seemed to make up his mind about something.

"Maya, I've been wanting to say something."

"Yes?" asked Maya. This sounded serious.

"I'm sorry. I think you were a little bit right about me, and I was wrong."

"About what?" asked Maya, mystified.

"About not going out in public with you. I think maybe I was avoiding it for some reason."

"Because you were embarrassed to be

seen with me?" asked Maya. It was an outrageous thing to be telling her, even if it was the truth.

"I hope not. I hope that wasn't the reason. But today, when I told Scotty we were going together, I liked saying it. I like *you*. And you don't deserve all the lies I've been telling you."

Despite the nice words, this sounded to Maya suspiciously like the preamble to being dumped. This was great. Her first date, she was stood up. Her second first date, and she's being dumped.

Kirk looked at the dashboard, and ran his finger around the steering wheel as he spoke. "The reason I didn't call you that night was because we don't have a phone," he said. "We don't have a phone because my dad didn't pay the bill, and I can't afford it. He didn't pay the bill because he doesn't have a job, and he drinks the welfare cheque. He doesn't work shifts, he drinks shifts — he's passed out by three o'clock every afternoon, gets up at eleven and passes out again by three in the morning. That night he was acting crazy, I was afraid he'd burn down the house or something."

Maya's mouth dropped open. She didn't know what to say. She'd heard of things like that, even read books about them. But she didn't know anyone it actually happened to, not that she knew of, anyway.

"But your mom?" she asked, tentatively.

"My mom," said Kirk, with a bitter edge Maya had never heard in his voice before. "My mom is gone. I don't know where she is. I barely even remember her. She probably couldn't take the old bum any more. I don't know why she thought I could."

Maya thought of her own mother, and couldn't picture her ever leaving her children behind anywhere. She reached out and put her hand on Kirk's arm. His eyes met hers.

"I don't want your pity, you know," he said evenly. "Just like you don't want mine. I just wanted you to know the truth."

Maya nodded.

"Lady Godiva's almost ready. She just needs a coat of paint. A couple more paycheques should do it."

Maya nodded again. Her first real date with Kirk shouldn't be making her feel so sad.

"That's the reason I'm leaving — because of my dad. I mean, I feel guilty because I can't seem to do anything for him, but then I feel mad because it shouldn't be up to me, and then I feel guilty for feeling mad. I think if I get to someplace new, I could start to be someone new."

"Won't you miss your friends?" asked

Maya. Again, she wanted to say, Won't you miss me?

"I don't have friends, I'm the lone wolf," Kirk said. "Don't get too close, and you can't get hurt, that's my philosophy. You know how it hurts when you pull off a Bandaid? Not if you don't stick it on in the first place."

"If you don't put on a Bandaid, you could get an infection, you heal slower," said Maya. "You need to have friends, even if they hurt you. Life's too big to carry by yourself." Maya thought of how she had needed Caitlin to help her through the stuff with Scotty, needed Kirk to help her win against him. She felt as churned up inside as if she had swallowed an electric mixer. Part of it was her heart breaking for Kirk, and part of it was feeling really touched that he trusted her so much to tell her all this. Part of it was selfishness, that she didn't want him to leave. And she wished he considered her a friend. And part of it was something else, that she couldn't define at all. Tears were brimming just below the surface.

"Don't go," she whispered, and Kirk gathered her into his arms. She buried her face in his shoulder. The fabric of his shirt was smooth, soft. He smelled of Ivory Soap. Maybe Kirk was right about the Bandaids. It did hurt.

"I have to," he said in a low voice. "I have to get away from my dad, at least for a while." Maya heard him swallow. "I promised myself I wouldn't let myself get hurt. Why did I have to meet you now?" Kirk pulled back and looked at her. "I'll miss you."

"Me too," said Maya. It was strange, this sensation that felt so bad and so good at the same time.

# Chapter 14

"Cheer up, Caitlin. At least we have a legitimate half-day off school," said Maya, as she neatly parallel-parked the van at a meter on Queen Street.

"Easy for you to say. You got your license on the very first try," moaned Caitlin.

"The instructor said it was my experience 'driving' the wheelchair, that's all. Anyway, you'll get yours next time. Third time lucky, right?"

"Bad things come in threes," responded Caitlin, gloomily.

"Well, cheer up anyway, 'cause we're celebrating *my* license, and it's my treat," replied Maya, transferring into her wheelchair. They had dropped off Maya's mom and Caitlin's dad, who had taken them to the test, and no doubt believed the girls were on their way back to school. Maya rolled down the ramp and locked the van, pulling her zippered sweater closer

147

around her. The leaves were golden and red in the brilliant sunshine, but Indian Summer had come and gone, and there was a distinct crispness to the air. Hallowe'en displays were in the windows of the shops as they made their way along the sidewalk toward Slurps.

Sarah Anne, who was finished school, was working on the counter and gave Maya a friendly hello as the girls came in the door.

"Hi, Sarah Anne," replied Maya. "This is my friend Caitlin. We're celebrating — I got my license!"

"And I didn't," said Caitlin, sounding a little more cheerful. "And she's buying."

"Way to go, Maya," said Sarah Anne, and then turned toward the kitchen. "Hey guys, look who's here." Tommy and Kei-Kei came out of the back together. There were a couple of people Maya didn't know, who remained in the kitchen.

"How's it going?" Tommy greeted her.

"Good," said Maya. "You know, school, the usual boring stuff."

"Yeah," Tommy laughed, and then lowered his voice. "Say, did you hear? Scotty got fired."

"He did? How do you know?" exclaimed Maya. She knew that because of her report, and Kirk's story corroborating it, something would happen. She had even received a letter a few weeks before, saying that "disciplinary action had been taken" and thanking her for coming forward. Presumably Kirk had been thanked too. But Scotty actually getting fired was the best news she could have heard.

"Grapevine," replied Kei-Kei to her question. "Heard from Kirk lately?" By the time Kirk had left, everyone at Slurps knew they were an item.

"Got a letter from him just the other day," said Maya. "He says hi to everyone. He's got a job cooking in a place called the Pacific Café in Vancouver, he says it's more like a restaurant than a snack bar, and the people who run it are really nice, and they have great calamari. He's sharing an apartment with two other guys, and he says he can see a teeny strip of water between the buildings across the way."

"Say hi to him from us," Tommy told her.

Maya didn't tell them about the rest of the letter. But as she and Caitlin went to their table, she ran over it in her mind — she had the whole letter completely memorized.

*I sent my dad some money, but I haven't heard from him. I hope he's all right.*

*It would all be so much nicer if yo*u

*were here. Black Beauty — Lady Godiva to you — misses you too. Sometimes on my day off, I take a drive up the coast. It's so beautiful, the mountains and the sea, and the islands, and I imagine that you're there with me. Maybe someday.*

*Love, Kirk*

*P.S. I've put something else in the envelope. I hope you remember me sometimes.*

Maya reached into her sweater pocket, slid her hand into the envelope the letter had come in. She smiled as she curled her fingers around the "something else" in the envelope. A Bandaid.

# About the Author

Kathryn Ellis has her own publicity company in Toronto, and among her clients are book publishing companies and the *Degrassi* television show. She has also written four scripts for *Degrassi*.

Kathryn grew up in Niagara Falls, Ontario, but also lived for nearly two years in Latin America. She graduated from Queen's University in Kingston, Ontario, with an honours degree in English. She and her husband live in Toronto — not too far from Degrassi Street — and she enjoys cooking, travelling and baseball.

Degrassi Books
based on the Degrassi Junior High/
Degrassi High TV Series

Exit Stage Left by *William Pasnak*
Stephanie Kaye by *Ken Roberts*
Spike by *Loretta Castellarin*
Shane by *Susin Nielsen*
Melanie by *Susin Nielsen*
Joey Jeremiah by *Kathryn Ellis*
Lucy by *Nazneen Sadiq*
Caitlin by *Catherine Dunphy*
Wheels by *Susin Nielsen*
Snake by *Susin Nielsen*
Maya by *Kathryn Ellis*
BLT by *Cathy Dunphy*